Hidden Truths

Hidden Truths

ELLY SWARTZ

DELACORTE PRESS

Text copyright © 2023 by Elly Swartz
Jacket art copyright © 2023 by Jen Bricking

All rights reserved. Published in the United States by Delacorte Press, an imprint of Random House Children's Books, a division of Penguin Random House LLC, New York.

Delacorte Press is a registered trademark and the colophon is a trademark of Penguin Random House LLC.

Visit us on the Web! rhcbooks.com

Educators and librarians, for a variety of teaching tools, visit us at RHTeachersLibrarians.com

Library of Congress Cataloging-in-Publication Data
Names: Swartz, Elly, author.
Title: Hidden truths / Elly Swartz.
Description: First edition. | New York : Delacorte Press, [2023] | Audience: Ages 8–12 years. |
Summary: Dani and Eric have been best friends since Dani moved next door in second grade—until one summer when everything changes.
Identifiers: LCCN 2022037919 (print) | LCCN 2022037920 (ebook) |
ISBN 978-0-593-48366-4 (hardcover) | ISBN 978-0-593-48367-1 (library binding) |
ISBN 978-0-593-48368-8 (ebook)
Subjects: CYAC: Best friends—Fiction. | Friendship—Fiction. | Accidents—Fiction. |
Baseball—Fiction.
Classification: LCC PZ7.1.S926 Hi 2023 (print) | LCC PZ7.1.S926 (ebook) | DDC [Fic]—dc23

The text of this book is set in 11.5-point Apollo MT Pro.
Interior design by Cathy Bobak

Printed in the United States of America
10 9 8 7 6 5 4 3 2 1
First Edition

For Joan—my sister, my best friend. This story is about the forever people in our lives. Grateful you are in mine.

1

Didn't Know

I didn't know today would matter.

I didn't know it would change everything.

I thought what mattered had already happened.

I was wrong.

2

Ostrich Legs

I squeeze the baseball in my hand and squint through my mirrored sunglasses at the sea of boys swirling around me. McKinnon stretches his long ostrich legs as he throws lefty to Braden. In the outfield are Billings, Henry, and some kid I don't recognize with a mouth full of red braces.

I stand on the pitching mound and close my eyes. I hear a lawn mower somewhere and breathe in a mix of grass and dirt, hoping it will calm the nerves marching up my spine. Today I find out if I made the baseball team.

I open my eyes and slide my left hand into the baseball glove I named Betty. The leather's worn and it molds around my fingers. I exhale and hear the buzz of boys talking and laughing, but I don't say a word. I can't. I don't want to jinx it.

Tryouts were held the morning I left for baseball camp. It had just rained, and the air was sticky. It was me and a pack of boys. All boys. Like always. But that day my arm was fire. Fastball after fastball landed smack in the catcher's mitt. I stand on the mound now, hoping that was enough.

Coach Levi said he'd be at the field by ten.

I swallow hard and look at my phone. It's 10:05.

I slip my phone back into my pocket and squeeze the baseball. The stitching feels good against my palm.

Then I see Coach Levi walking across the field. My stomach flips.

As he gets closer, the kids scattered around the field move like a swarm toward the dugout.

Please let this be good news.

"Well, hello, everyone," Coach says, taking off his cap and running his hand over his buzz cut.

The clouds roll in front of the sun, and I move my sunglasses to the top of my head.

He claps his hands together. "I asked you all to the field because I wanted to congratulate you on making the Mapleville fall baseball team."

The words linger in the air. Shock floods my brain, followed by a tidal wave of happiness.

After years of blah, blah, blah—"You're good for a girl, but not good enough to make the team"—I finally did it!

Coach talks about the game and the practice schedule, and when he finishes, everyone erupts into cheers and high fives. And I'm part of it.

I quickly text Eric the news.

Then the team lines up and Coach hands out our uniforms. I toss my new navy-and-red Mapleville shirt over my tank top and stuff my long brown frizzle of hair into my team hat. Coach talks about working hard and supporting each other, and then says he'll see us for practice next week.

My first official team meeting is over, and my heart is dancing.

When I look up, Eric's leaning his mountain bike against the fence by the field.

I run over. We haven't seen each other since I left for baseball camp a month ago. I got back this morning, just before Coach sent the email telling us to meet at the field.

"Welcome home!" he bursts out, his dimple showing.

I smile. "Thanks," I say, glancing over my shoulder at my team. "Can you believe it? I finally got picked!"

"Totally believe it," he says, taking something out of his backpack. "Your fastball's a beast."

"Yeah, but that's never been enough. At least until now!" I pause as a neon-green Frisbee flies across the next field. "I'm excited you're here. You look taller."

He flexes his skinny arms. "And stronger."

I laugh. "I didn't think you'd come to the field. I mean, I'm seeing you later for our camping trip."

"I know, but since you made the team, I had to bring donuts to celebrate." He swipes his floppy curls to the side and holds up a bakery box.

I'm about to reach for a Boston cream when I hear McKinnon call my name. I turn around.

He's standing in front of the boy pack, waving me over. "Team's going for pizza."

"Oh," Eric says, rapid blinking. "Yeah, I mean, you should go with them."

I look at my team in their Mapleville shirts and caps, and then back at Eric. I yell to McKinnon, "I'll meet you there."

Eric stares at me. "Go. It's cool, I'll see you later."

"You sure?"

He nods.

"Will you save me a donut?" I ask.

He tilts his head and raises an eyebrow. "No promises."

I laugh. "That's fair."

Eric hops on his bike.

"Hey, thanks for coming and for the almost-donut and for understanding how big this is." I talk fast like I might explode with joy. "You're the best!"

He nods.

"After this team thing, I'll pack super quick and meet you at your house for the camping trip," I tell him. "I want to hear about all the things I missed while I was at baseball camp."

He gives me a thumbs-up.

"I made the team!" I shout as I wave good-bye. "I can't even believe I finally get to say those words!"

I'm still floating from the news when I get home. Pizza with the team was kind of awkward at first, then mostly normal and fun. I didn't know that good news could make my brain feel fizzy like cream soda. I race up to my room to pack. I promised Eric I'd be speedy.

The sun slides through my shutters. It hits my yellow shag carpet in the perfect rectangle. My golden retriever, Casey, wags her tail and stretches her giant fluff of a body across the sun-filled spot. She watches as I crank up the music, dance around my room, and open my duffel bag.

Thank goodness she's a dog and can't record any of this on a phone.

When the song ends, I toss in Betty, a pair of flip-flops, my super cute striped bathing suit, the SPF 80 sunblock and bug spray Mom's forcing me to bring, a rainbow beach towel, my Mapleville baseball sweatshirt, a deck of cards, and a few other random things for my mostly annual camping trip with Eric. We skipped it last year. My grandma Gigi had died that spring, and instead of fishing and swimming and being eaten by mosquitoes the weekend before middle school started, we hung out in Eric's tree fort reading comics, eating donuts, and talking about forever people.

I think he could tell that my heart was heavy—and not because he didn't get that Mystique was actually the greatest comic book character of all time, but because good-byes are hard. That was the day I learned that donuts and comic books and friends can't fix everything.

I look in the full-length mirror dangling on the back of my closet door, smile at my team gear, and twirl the coin in my pocket.

Eric gave it to me that weekend in the tree fort. He'd just devoured his glazed donut in two bites and was doing a terrible job convincing me that Iron Man was the best superhero ever. Then he reached into his pocket and handed me the coin. He said I should have it, that it always brought him luck—and that he was sorry it was sweaty.

I flip the coin one more time. It's over a year later, and I still like having it with me.

I glance around my room, making sure I didn't forget anything for the camping trip. I tuck in the corners of my quilt one more time so they're just right. Straighten the home run baseball that sits on my yellow desk next to the fake plant that Mom got for me after I killed two real ones and a cactus.

I grab my duffel. As I walk past the skinny glass table where Mom dumps her keys, I see my favorite photo of me and Eric at the Red Sox game eating hot dogs with heaps of relish.

Happiness floods my brain, and I realize how much I missed my friend with the skinny arms and the terrible taste in superheroes.

3
Rainbow Popsicles

"Eric, you're late." Dad's gravelly voice echoes up the wooden stairs.

I hop off my crossword app, stuff the dirty clothes scattered across my floor into my bag, and put the sadly unfinished superhero comic on the shelf in the back of the closet. My Avengers T-shirt passes the smell test, so I throw it on. It swallows my arms even though I've been doing push-ups all summer.

I sprint downstairs. Dani and her dog, Casey, are already in the kitchen, surrounded by one of Mom's worst decisions: the pink-and-orange paisley wallpaper. I run over and give Dani a giant congratulations hug—something that was definitely not happening at the field in front of the guys—and realize she's got more freckles and smells different. Like flowers. Or something fruity.

I'm about to ask her what it is when she says, "Thanks for understanding before."

"Yeah. No problem." I turn around, stuffing away any leftover crumbs of disappointment, then spin back toward her. "The real question is how much you missed me while you were away!" I laugh.

She stretches out her arms.

"I knew it!" I say, grabbing a banana from the ceramic fruit bowl on the counter.

Dani smiles. "Baseball camp was pretty awesome, though. And then coming home and finding out I made the team was epic!"

We break into the victory dance we've been doing since we won rainbow popsicles in second grade for coming in first in the neighborhood's Fourth of July potato sack race.

We're still dancing around the table when Mom walks in. "Nice to see that nothing's changed," she says. "Happy you're back, Dani. We've missed you around here, and congrats on making the team!"

"Thanks," Dani says.

"You guys ready?" Dad's holding a white foam cooler and a grocery bag I'm hoping is full of chips.

I nod.

"Maybe double-check your bag to make sure you haven't forgotten anything," he says, walking out the front door.

"Nope. I'm good."

"You brought your glove, right?" Dani asks, petting Casey, who's trying to nose her way closer to an open jar of peanut butter.

"Why do I need my glove? Thought we were just fishing and swimming, like always. I even perfected my cannonball while you were gone."

"Coach says I should practice every day."

"Okay, but you remember what happened last summer?"

She makes a face. "That was an accident."

After her Gigi died, Dani didn't want to do much of anything but play baseball. So one day I dragged her giant red bucket of baseballs to the field and told her she could pitch to me. That was the day I learned about hand-eye coordination. And how I don't have any.

I dart upstairs and dig my baseball glove from the wicker basket in the corner that still smells like the turkey jerky I accidentally left in there last week. As I'm leaving my room, I run into my five-year-old sister, Zoe.

"I'm going to miss you." She wraps her arms tight around my waist.

"I'll miss you too, Peanut," I say.

Then I grab my bag and race out the door to meet Dani and my dad in our white-and-brown camper. Dad got it like a month ago. Said it was in mint condition, with only twenty thousand miles on it.

"This is so cool," Dani says, running her fingers along the countertop. "Whoa! It has a refrigerator and a stove and a bed *and* a bathroom." She pauses. "Have to admit, I'm pretty happy there's an actual toilet and not a porta potty, like we used on our other camping trips. Those stink worse than rotten cheese and vomit together."

I laugh. "And check this out." I hold up a white-and-brown mini remote-control version of our camper. "Dad found it at Big Al's Consignment Shop."

"Nice!"

"Right? I just need to charge it." I plug the remote-control camper into the outlet in the back and point to the bench by the kitchen table. "There's also this cool diner booth in one of the many shades of brown."

Dani glances around at the brown counters, brown kitchen cabinets, and brown flowered seat cushions. "Yeah, what's with all the brown?"

I shrug and throw my backpack onto the bench. "At least our sleeping bags are blue."

Dad gets behind the wheel and glances back at us. "Seems we're missing a passenger."

Dani and I look at each other and yell, "Find me!"

In two minutes, Casey's jumping into the camper with muddy paws, searching for the cheesy dog treat Dani's holding behind her back. We crack up as we pull out of the driveway.

After an hour and a lot of Dani texting the baseball team, we get to the Sagamore Bridge. We both open our windows. The Cape Cod air floods the camper, and the canal stretches below us. Casey sticks her head out the window, feeling the breeze as we drive across the bridge. I take a giant breath in.

This is our favorite part.

The moment we cross over.

4

Like a Good Secret

The dirt road to our campsite is long and winding and anchored by a line of pines and oak trees that salute us like soldiers as we pass. The camper rattles and sways as the tires kiss the potholes left over from the snowy winter. Feels like we're driving to nowhere. Like we're lost. But I know we're not. I stare out the window, and behind the mass of trees is the campground and then the lake—tucked away like a good secret. I inhale deep.

Eric knocks my flip-flop with his sneaker. "Ready for the best weekend of the year?"

I nod and smile.

Mr. Stein finds our campsite and parks. "We're here!"

He stands and stretches and his mostly bald head nearly hits the top of the camper. "I need to check us in at the camp office. You guys are in charge of hanging the lanterns and gathering firewood for tonight."

"Got it," Eric says. Then to me, "Swim first?"

"Yep, let's do it." I take out my phone. "I just need to send this pic of Casey with the two baseballs in her mouth to the team chat. They're picking a mascot."

Eric doesn't say anything, which is a little weird, since he's the one who actually took the photo.

I hit Send and grab my bathing suit from my bag.

"Reminder, sunblock and bug spray before either of you go out, or I'll be in big trouble with both moms," Mr. Stein says as he leaves the camper.

I douse my body with the required block and spray, then hop into the bathroom to change. It's small and everything is the color of mud, but it's private. I slip into my new one-piece and put my team hat back on, and when I look in the mirror, I'm happy from my head to my flip-flops.

I step out and see Eric sitting at the table in the same Avengers swimsuit he's been wearing for two years, making his way through a family-size bag of Doritos. I grab a handful of chips, and we head to the lake, Casey following us.

On the way, we pass a couple reading in Adirondack chairs and a family of five making s'mores around a firepit.

"I could eat this air," Eric says. "Seriously, it smells like marshmallows."

I laugh.

We follow the dirt path behind the row of campers to the water. Picnic tables are sprinkled everywhere. A few squirrels dart in front of us to retrieve the half-eaten hot dog someone dropped on the ground, but Casey gets there first. In the background I hear voices coming from the lake. Then Eric turns to me. "Last one in has to go back and get the towels I forgot."

He runs ahead and leaps off the dock into the water. I sigh and spin around toward the camper. I've been collecting stuff Eric's forgotten since I moved next door to him in second grade. I grab the towels from the table, then sprint to the water. Casey's swimming in circles and Eric's floating on his back as I race down the dock and cannonball over his head.

"Okay, I'll give you an eight out of ten for that one," Eric says. "Mostly because you didn't land on me."

"Ha! That was a solid ten," I say as the water shoots a cold blast right through me.

We float and jump and swim until our fingers look like raisins. Then we climb out of the water and lie on the dock to warm up. Kayaks are stacked on a rack alongside a shed nearby. The door's open, and I spy boogie boards and a pile of life jackets. Swimming lessons for a group of little kids in water wings just ended, so we're alone except for the girl with long braids sitting on the lifeguard stand. I wonder if she lives in one of the pretty cottages along the lake's edge.

I stare at the blue sky. The sun feels good on my cold body until my dog shakes her wet fur all over me.

"Casey!" I jump up and start laughing. "Well, I guess I'm dry enough. Want to get the firewood?"

Eric nods, his now-dry curls hanging in his eyes. "Hey, I'm really glad we're back here."

"Yeah, me too," I say, nudging his shoulder. "I kind of forgot how much I love this place."

Casey runs ahead to the trail into the woods like she's searching for the rest of the hot dog. The leaves and dirt and pine needles create a soft cushion beneath my feet as I grab different-sized sticks for the fire. I spy a nest with a mama bird and her babies. I'm about to show Eric when I see him ducking behind a large pine.

I shake my head and walk over. "What are you doing?"

"Shhh," he says, pointing to someone in the distance.

I see a kid way taller than me with spiky black hair, and I know what's going on. I exhale and step out from behind the tree.

Eric pulls at my arm. "Don't," he whispers loudly.

But I wriggle free and walk closer and closer to the kid.

When the kid turns, I see his round, sunburned cheeks, his CELTICS RULE T-shirt, and his shiny silver earring.

I wave awkwardly. "Oh, um, sorry. Thought you were someone else."

"It's cool," he says, moving past me.

I head back to Eric. "You can breathe. It's not him."

Eric steps out from the behind the tree and kicks the dirt. "Oh. And, um, thanks."

"You can't hide every time you see or *think* you see Leo."

A rabbit darts past us, and Casey takes off after it.

"I know." Eric stares down at the ground. "But we've seen his family camping here before."

I nod.

"And this is the last weekend before school starts, and I don't want to run into him."

"Maybe it won't be like before. Maybe he's not as big a jerk. You know, people can change."

Eric's quiet. "I guess," he says finally. "But he hasn't. Not since that time I bumped into him, his brother, and his dad in Shopmart. Remember? My mom was holding a pack of Iron Man boxers. I was maybe six or seven and tried to deny they were mine, but it's not like I have brothers. And they weren't exactly my dad's size."

"Well, the good news is you're not still wearing superhero boxers," I say, laughing a little. "Right?"

Eric frowns. "It's only gotten worse over the years, and I'm sick of being picked on and made fun of and him totally getting away with it. And it doesn't help that each year he seems to grow five more inches and I, well, don't."

My heart hurts for my friend. "Look, whatever happens at school with Leo this year, I've got your back. I promise."

"Yeah, thanks."

We finish gathering the wood and dump the pile of sticks by the firepit.

"Baseball?" I ask.

He shakes his head. "Let's hang the lanterns before my dad thinks I forgot. Then catch dinner. I don't want his version of spaghetti." I stick out my tongue in agreement. Mr. Stein insists it's a secret recipe, but Eric and I both know it's really just noodles with ketchup.

We string the happy-face lanterns between the two oak trees next to our camper. Then we grab our fishing rods and earthworms and walk back across the stretch of pebbles to the lake's gravelly edge.

"Just want you to know," Eric says, threading the worm onto his hook, "this is *the* year."

"For what?" I ask.

"Talking to Rachel." He casts his line way out. "I even signed up for that club she's part of."

"I thought the plan was that you were going to speak to her this summer while I was at baseball camp." I wiggle my line. Eric's had a crush on Rachel since the fourth grade.

"It was. But every time I bumped into her, she was with a group of kids. Except the last time, and I was with Zoe."

"What's wrong with being with Zoe?"

"She puked butterscotch ice cream all over the sidewalk and my shoes."

I laugh.

"Not funny," he says, and then laughs with me.

His line tightens. "Oooh. I think I got one."

Eric tilts, pulls, and sways until he reels in a big fat trout.

We high five and bring our prize fish to Eric's dad, who cleans it, sprinkles it with some Old Bay seasoning, wraps it in tinfoil, and cooks it over an open fire. That was always Gigi's job on the camping trip. Not the cleaning but the cooking.

The smell of fish edges out the smell of marshmallows while we eat. I take a bite and realize that Eric's dad is a way better fish cleaner than fish cook. Which makes me miss Gigi. But I don't say anything. I've gotten used to missing her. Which makes me sad in other ways.

I swat a mosquito off my leg, share the rest of my trout with Casey, and sneak a peek at the team's group chat on my phone. Juan just sent a photo of his guinea pig, named Big Papi. I'm replying with a picture of Casey wearing a baseball cap when I hear someone clearing his throat. I look up.

It's Eric's dad. "I promised your mom that you wouldn't be on the phone the whole time."

"But it's about the team mascot." I show him my phone. "You have to admit, Casey would make the best mascot."

"Agreed, but I promised. So why don't you hit Send and then put it away for a bit."

He pauses. The half-moon casts a hazy light around him. "You know, we're so proud that you made the team, Dani."

"Thanks," I say, rubbing the fur between Casey's ears.

Mr. Stein grabs the dishes and heads inside the camper.

"Ready?" Eric asks as a firefly dances around him.

"Maybe we skip it this time," I say.

"Because you're scared?"

"No, because ghost stories are for little kids."

Eric laughs. "That's not a thing."

I blow out a breath of frustration.

Eric lowers his voice and whispers the words real slow: "The air was hot and sticky when Jameson crawled out of bed."

I hear a branch snap and tuck my knees close to my chest. The fire burns between us. When Eric's done telling his ghost story, my body sits frozen while my breath searches for its normal rhythm.

"Well, what do you think?" Eric asks in his back-to-normal voice.

I straighten my legs. "Wow. That was, like, top-five good."

"Thanks," he says, swatting a mosquito away from his arm.

I stand up.

"Where are you going?"

"My foot fell asleep." I hop around, trying to wake it. "And I kind of thought we were done."

Eric's face falls. "But we haven't had mac and cheese or the donuts I brought from home."

"I'm pretty tired," I say, which is mostly true.

Eric nudges the ground with his sneaker, stirring up bits

of grass and dirt. "But we always have donuts and mac and cheese on the first night of our camping trip." His voice sounds small.

I don't say anything.

"Why are you being so weird about this?" he asks. "It's mac and cheese and a donut. It'll take five minutes for me to inhale."

"How can you still be hungry?"

"Growth spurt," he says, flexing his barely-there biceps.

I look at my friend with the skinny arms and realize again how much I missed him. He's the one person who knows all of me. That I hate cantaloupe, sleep with my closet light on, and sometimes feel stuck in a quicksand of sad. "All right."

A goofy smile spreads across Eric's face. "You grab the donuts. They're in the box on top of my duffel. Just be quiet—my dad's probably asleep," he says. "I'll make the mac and cheese and bring it out when it's done."

I get the donuts and throw on my team sweatshirt. Casey follows me to the firepit. Fog has rolled in. I wrap myself in one of the fuzzy fleece blankets Mr. Stein left for us and check the team text. Nothing new. I put my phone away and wait until Eric brings out two tin mugs of mac and cheese.

We sit and eat donuts and mac and cheese, surrounded by a rainbow of happy-face lanterns and a sky filled with stars that flicker against the black night.

A perfect end to a perfect day.

5

The Sound of Nothing

I wake before the sun rises and have to pee. A note taped to one of the brown camper cabinets says Dad's fishing and will be back soon to make breakfast. My stomach grumbles at the thought of two fried eggs with cheesy goodness on top. Dani's still sleeping and has rolled in front of the bathroom, totally blocking the door. I try to wake her or move her and the sleeping bag out of the way, but neither budges. The tile floor is stone-cold on my bare feet, so I wrap a blanket around my body and head outside into the fog. *Ouch!* A sharp rock jabs my big toe. I look around to make sure no one's nearby, then pee behind some pines.

I'm walking back toward the camper when I hear a

thundering *boom!* Like a loud crash. I reach up to cover my ears.

The ground shakes under my toes, and my head throbs. The sound lingers.

What is that?

I feel heat.

I look up.

And start screaming.

Yellow and red flames shoot out from a broken window at the back of the camper.

"Dani!" I yell, tripping over my blanket, falling knee-first onto some rocks. The crisp morning air morphs into a stew of black smoke. I see flames lapping at the far end of the camper. I get up and run for the door.

Inside, paper, bits of plastic, and other stuff fly in the air like confetti. "Dani!" My eyes burn. I cough. Bang into something. Gasp. Run out the door to grab air. My fingers are laced with soot. Blood trickles down my leg. I dart into the camper again. Crouch low. That's when I see Dani lying on the floor, pinned under some cabinets and the bathroom door.

I give her a little shake. She groans but doesn't move. I push and shove and finally inch the toppled cabinets off of her.

The fire's in the back for now, but the burning smell makes me gag. I don't want to hurt her more but I have to get her out of here. I pull Dani from the camper and lay her on the ground. An adult in a uniform runs over and kneels beside her. He's holding her hand while someone puts a clear mask on her face, squeezing a bag of air into her mouth. A man with a white mustache brings a fire extinguisher. A woman with a baseball cap directs campers away from the area.

Dad runs toward me.

He's yelling something and his arms are flailing. I see his mouth move but can't hear anything. Then he hugs me.

My body shakes with fear. I pull out of Dad's arms, clutch my stomach, and puke.

My dad's mouth moves, but I still can't hear. Feels like I'm trapped inside one of the video games Mom's always telling me to stop playing.

Dad wraps his arms around me.

Silence.

He pulls back and mouths something else to me.

No sound.

Fear spreads across his face.

I take a deep breath and close my eyes. The sound of nothingness calms me. Maybe none of this is real.

Then, "Eric, can you hear me?"

I open my eyes, and just like that, the silence is gone and chaos closes in.

I see Dani. The official-looking people hover over her. Her leg's twisted and bent in a not-normal way.

A woman in a flowered sweatshirt frantically scoops up

a screaming kid in pajamas. Cell phones buzz and sing, but the tunes are swallowed by scattered screams and the rush of water spraying from a hose.

"Eric, are you all right?" Dad repeats. He's crying.

I nod.

"Thank goodness you're okay," he says. Then, as if to make sure: "Do you know who I am? Where we are?"

"Yes." My voice cracks as I stare at the flames shooting out the back of the camper.

Dad wipes the soot from my hands and the blood from the knee I forgot was cut. More chaos.

I go toward Dani, but Dad holds me back. "Not right now, Eric. Let them help her."

I stare at Dani. *Is she breathing?* I can't tell. I mean, I think she is, but I don't know. I shove away the horrible-never-say-out-loud possibilities and pray.

I'll do anything, please just let Dani be okay.

I stink at praying.

I try again.

I'll set two alarms in the mornings. Never oversleep again. Clean my room. Remember stuff. Anything.

Finally, Dani coughs.

My heart resets.

Thank you.

I drag my blackened hand across my forehead and mop up the sticky sweat.

Dani is screaming something about her leg.

My body wobbles. "She's going to be okay, right?" I ask my dad. Two fire engines, a ladder truck, and an ambulance roar onto the site, sirens screaming.

"I hope so," he says, using his shirt to wipe the red stains off me.

That's not the answer I want.

6

Drift and Float

Sounds are muffled and loud. In and out.

"Dani, I'm Jefferson. I work at the campground. The ambulance is here to take you to the hospital."

I hear the voice. Sort of.

More sounds. More words.

But they drift and float. Then they're lost.

I wonder if this is what *almost* feels like.

I can almost hear. Almost feel. Almost grasp what's happening.

I try to move but pain shoots from everywhere. My body feels heavy, like the red tub of baseballs.

The air feels cold. Or is that me? Am I shivering?

My mind closes. Darkness folds around me. I'm tired. Really tired.

More noise. More heaviness.

I drift.

7

Back to the Before

"I need to be with Dani," I tell my dad. "Please." I lean against the trunk of an oak tree to steady myself. Dirt-covered tears roll down my cheeks.

"You can't, Eric. Not now. The EMTs are putting her in the ambulance. We'll follow them. You have to get checked by a doctor, too."

I shake my head. "I'm fine. What I need is to be with Dani."

My dad hugs me.

Worry drifts down my neck.

Somewhere a dog barks.

I look around. "Where's Casey?" I ask, my voice laced

with fear as I watch the firefighters douse the flames with powerful streams of water.

Was Casey in the camper? Did she come outside with me?

I dig through my brain but don't remember.

"Casey!" I yell.

Dani's dog can't be in there. I shake my head back and forth. *No. No. No.* Then I race toward the camper. A firefighter in a helmet and a large black jacket with neon-yellow stripes moves in front of the door. "You can't go in there. It's not safe."

"But my friend's dog. She may be . . . I don't know. But . . ." My words trail off.

"Eric, take a deep breath," Dad says, guiding me away from the camper.

"I have to find Dani's dog. This is the one thing—the *only* thing—I can do for her."

"Let's think it through together. Okay?" Dad says.

I nod as the tears slip down my face.

"Did Casey follow you out of the camper this morning?" He rests his hand on my shoulder.

I close my eyes. Think back to before. The cold floor. Dani asleep in front of the bathroom door. Me stepping out of the camper. Stubbing my toe. *Is Casey with me? Does she nudge my hand with her cold nose?* I squeeze my eyes shut, trying to see what my brain can't.

"I don't remember." I start calling for her.

Dad follows.

We run through the thick forest on the left. The pine needles coat the path, but their scent is gone, replaced with fire and smoke and fear.

I didn't know fear had a smell.

Until now.

We run down to the lake—Casey's favorite spot. I yell for her. Nothing.

I run toward the oak trees on the right, past the now-abandoned firepits, picnic tables, and campsites. "Casey, come!" My voice is scratchy. I dig in my pocket for treats. But it's empty except for an old tissue and a crumpled gum wrapper.

I stop running and look up. *Please let Dani and Casey be okay. Please. I'll do more chores. I'll clean out Dad's toolshed and stinky fishing stuff. Whatever you want.*

My heart pounds.

Dad catches up with me.

Blood from my knee drips down my leg. "I don't understand what happened," I say, looking around at what was supposed to be the best weekend of the summer.

"I don't know. But I do know we need to get you to the hospital." He rips the bottom part off his T-shirt and ties it around my cut. "The firefighters are here. They can look for Casey and keep us informed."

I freeze. *Informed* sounds like a word soaked in horrible things.

"Dad, we have to find Casey," I say, desperation leaking into every word.

He shakes his head. "Eric, it's not a good idea."

"Please."

He sighs. "For now, but if that gash gets worse, we're leaving."

I nod, trying to ignore the throbbing.

We race down another dirt path. "Casey!" I yell.

Then I hear it. A rustle of leaves. I turn around.

A squirrel runs away.

Not Casey.

I exhale and keep calling. And running. And searching. I go down another path, this one filled with thorns and honeysuckles.

"Come on, girl."

Time slips. I keep going. I can't stop moving, because I don't want Dad to tell me we have to leave. I need to do this for Dani.

"Find me!" I yell.

Another rustle of leaves.

I turn around.

But this time it's not a squirrel.

This time it's Casey.

Running toward me.

8

Like Static

Someone is talking. A woman.

"Mom? Is that you?"

No answer. More talking. Lots of voices. Crisscrossing.

Muffled together.

Like static.

Buzzing.

Sounds fading.

It's cold and I'm tired. I close my eyes. Wait, are they already closed? Am I sleeping? Where am I?

My thoughts weave and wander.

I'm pitching. My lucky coin is in my pocket. I throw a strike. And then another. And another. I look around. But no one's here. I'm alone. No batter. No team.

Where did everybody go?

9
Jitter Bob

I hug Dani's wet dog, who smells like smoke. She licks my face, and Dad wraps us in his big arms. Lloyd the EMT comes over and cleans the cut on my knee, squeezes some ointment on it, and wraps it in gauze. Then he offers us a ride to the hospital. I sit in the back seat of his muddied truck, and Casey lays her body across my lap. It feels good, having her near me. My mind spins as I stare at the fly sitting on the pizza box next to me.

Okay, God, it's me again. Thanks for before. And I don't mean to sound ungrateful, but I kind of need something else. I need Dani to be okay-okay. As in totally fine. Please.

I hear Dad talking to Mom on the phone. She's with Alice, Dani's mom. They're driving to the hospital now.

I rub behind Casey's ears like I'm helping somehow.

My eyes feel heavy, but I'm too scared to close them. Too scared to see what I saw. Feel what I felt.

When we pull into the hospital parking lot, Aunt Josie's waiting for us. She lives halfway between home and the Cape and drives way too fast, so she got here quick.

"You frightened me," Aunt Josie says, wiping a tear she doesn't want me to see. "I love you." She grabs my face in her hands. I spy her missing tooth. Josie's terrified of the dentist. She's also afraid of spiders and the color teal. Thankfully, she's not afraid of dogs and has agreed to watch Casey until we're done at the hospital.

"Love you, too, Aunt Josie. I promise, I'm okay."

She hugs me. "I'm putting it out in the world to heal Dani."

"Thanks." Aunt Josie believes if you say your wish out loud—put it into the world—it'll come true.

I love that about her. She does everything a little sideways. Like me, I guess. She always says we're a lot alike, both skinny, scattered, smart, and full of laughter. I like the smart and laughter parts.

"And, um, I appreciate your watching Casey."

"I'm happy to help. Plus, Casey can keep Charles company."

I rub Casey's ears, wish her luck with Charles—Aunt Josie's ancient hairless cat—and kiss her cold nose before we go into the hospital.

As soon as the automatic hospital doors open, the smell of sickness hits me in the face. It's like rubbing alcohol and puke mixed with feet and bad breath.

I try not to breathe but eventually lose that battle. Then Dad and I are brought back to a room in the ER with a divider that reminds me of the blue shower curtain at home. Which isn't great, since I have to wear a hospital gown that opens in the back. I ask for two so I can keep everything covered. The doctor comes in and examines me. Turns out the gash on my knee from falling on the rocks is just a bad cut that needs cleaning, more antiseptic, and a large Band-Aid.

When I'm done, Mom's waiting for Dad and me with clean clothes. Her eyes are red. She holds me tight.

The morning feels like a movie in fast-forward—everything speeding past me, too fast to fully understand.

Mom traces her hand down my cheek.

"Mom, I'm all right." I pull back. "The doctor even said so."

We walk along the white-walled hallway with strange hospital smells to the waiting room and sit in the rigid orange plastic chairs. Life-size cutouts of Spider-Man, Batman, and Superman stare at me, and the music from *Beauty and the Beast* plays through a speaker above my head.

Hey, God, about that Dani thing, just a reminder in case you forget stuff like me: Please make sure she's okay.

My brain wanders to a little over a month ago. It was the night before Dani left for baseball camp. We sat at the counter seats at Harry's Hot Dog Palace and got hot dogs with heaps of relish and an order of curly fries to share. I look around the stale waiting room and wish we were back there now.

My eyes sting and my hands still smell like smoke.

Mom leans over after a few minutes. "You must be hungry. Why don't we take a walk to the cafeteria?" She stands up.

I sigh. She's not totally wrong. I am hungry, but more than that, my worries need space. I need space. To breathe. "I'll go myself."

Mom glances at my dad. I interject before he flanks my other side—I've seen them do the silent tag-team parent thing before—"I'll be fine. I promise."

My parents look at each other again and then at me. They have a weird unspoken conversation, then Dad hands me food money and gives me directions to the cafeteria.

I weave through the halls—each one a different shade of happy colors. At the end of the kiwi-green one, I find the cafeteria. I grab a bagel and a carton of chocolate milk and slide into a table next to a couple holding hands. Someone left today's *Clippings* on the table with the crossword puzzle half filled in. Something else I have in common with Aunt Josie. She's the original family crossword puzzle master.

The clue for 22 down: "Chase away, as a fly." I fill in SHOO. For 18 across: "Tiger____." The answer: WOODS. I finish most of the puzzle, check my phone for news about Dani. No word yet. I stare at the food and realize that no matter how hungry I am, I can't eat anything. I get up and head back.

I take the pumpkin-orange corridor that dead-ends at the hospital chapel. Wrong way. I stand there but don't turn around. Instead I peek inside. The room is dimly lit, with candles and red velvet seats and pews.

I wonder if I need to be more religious to go inside.

I look down at my soot-covered sneakers.

Or dressed nicer.

Or cleaner.

I stare through the stained-glass window to see if there's a dress code posted, but there isn't.

A woman with wrinkles around her eyes and blue-rimmed glasses walks out. "Bless you, my child," she says as she passes me.

Am I supposed to bless her back?

I whisper, "Bless you, too," in case that's a thing people do. I pull the door open and step inside. *Breathe.* It's small and kind of like my temple. Not the Torah part, but the pulpit, the soft seats, and the stained-glass window. I don't feel strange or out of place, which is weird. Not that I go to

40

Shabbat services every week, but I thought I'd feel like an outsider in this chapel. But I don't. I slip into a seat in the back, clasp my hands together, squeeze my eyes shut, hoping I'm doing this right, and pray. Again.

I re-promise to clean my room and Dad's shed if Dani's all right.

Can I repeat a prayer? Is that how this works?

In case I need a new one, I promise to stop drinking the milk straight from the half-gallon carton in the refrigerator.

My mind drifts. What happened this morning? I replay everything we did when we got to the Cape. We collected firewood, fished, and cannonballed off the dock. We swam until our fingers looked like raisins, strung the lights, ate dinner, told ghost stories, made mac and cheese, and finished off the donuts.

As I'm staring at the stained-glass window, it hits me like a burst of freezing water in the shower. The stove! Dad's always lecturing me about the danger of leaving it on. He reminded me, like, a thousand times before he even let me use it myself. Last night I turned it on to boil the milk to make the mac and cheese.

What if I never shut off the stove?

I feel all the air seep out of the chapel.

I forget stuff all the time.

Last night Dani and I were talking about my plan to finally talk to Rachel. What if I got distracted and forgot to shut off the stove?

What if this is my fault?

Dani didn't even want the mac and cheese. She wanted to go to sleep.

Beads of sweat race down my back. I interlock my hands until my knuckles turn bone white, get down on my knees, and amend my prayer.

God, I'm back.

My breath is stiff and choppy.

Please make Dani all right and make this not my fault.

I need air.

I walk out of the chapel and find a bathroom. Splash water on my face and dry it with a brown paper towel that smells like wet dog and chemicals. I stare at myself in the mirror.

What did I do?

I weave back to the waiting room, which now includes a woman talking way too loudly on her cell phone about Buttons—her neighbor's cat—and a couple sharing a bag of Doritos.

Mom's sipping coffee and Dad's doing something on his phone. They look up when I walk over. "Did you find food?" Dad asks, foot tapping.

"Mm-hmm." My brain is on guilt overload. I sit down but stand up again when I can't stop my knee from bouncing. Mom calls it my jitter bob. She says Aunt Josie has it, too, and when they watch *Jeopardy!* together, the couch shakes.

I pace until my leg stops, then push a couple of chairs together and slide in my earbuds, hoping the music drowns out the shouting in my head.

But it doesn't.

Your fault.

Your fault.

Your fault.

10
Just Me

I feel Mom's hand in mine. It's buttery soft and holding tight.

I open my eyes. She slides her hand out.

"Hey, kiddo." She's wearing her LIFE'S A PICKLE sweatshirt.

My lips are dry. She gives me a spoon and a cup with ice chips. "This should help."

Her smile's warm.

Her steel-blue eyes are worried.

"Thanks," I say, my voice raspy. I notice the white walls and bright lights in my hospital room. Machines beep as I survey my space. My body doesn't look or feel like my body. My right leg is in a blue cast from knee to ankle and is hanging in a hammock-like thing. My head is foggy. My right shoulder is purply black, and my right hand feels tingly and numb.

"How long have I been sleeping?" My throat is like sandpaper.

Mom looks at her phone. "Since they brought you to the room. About an hour or so."

"I can't believe I was camping this morning."

Mom exhales and rests her hand on the metal railing on the side of my bed. "Dr. Jeffries was in earlier. Do you remember him?"

I nod. My neck feels stiff. "Yeah. He was the guy with the purple bow tie. Said I fractured my tibia, then he put a cast on the bottom part of my leg." I stare at my body. "What's the plan now?"

Mom glances at the notes on her yellow lined pad. "They need to run some more tests on your shoulder."

I try to wriggle my fingers but can't. I mean, my brain is telling them to move, but they're just lying there, not listening.

Worry slides in.

"What's, um, wrong with my hand?" A nervous knot ties in my stomach. "Why can't I move it?"

"Dr. Jeffries said you sustained nerve damage in your shoulder. He hopes it will improve when the swelling goes down."

Hopes?

"Dani, honey, the most important thing to remember, the only thing that truly matters, is that you're okay." She smiles, then barely takes a breath before diving back into whatever else she wrote on her pad. "And with a fractured tibia, you can gradually bear weight with the cast on. Then, if all goes well, in around two months, the cast comes off, you get a boot, and from there just lots of PT to get strong." She talks like this is a winning plan.

But my head spins. "Two months?"

She nods and keeps going. "However, Dr. Jeffries said with the nerve damage you likely won't be able to grip crutches initially."

I blow out a big breath. "Then how do I get around?"

"You'll mostly use *that* while you're here and at school." She points to the wheelchair parked at the end of my bed.

My brain is on overload.

"But when you get home, you get to use the rolling walker." It's in the corner. It has some weird arm attachment and looks more like something Gigi would have used.

Mom glances up from her notes. "Dr. Jeffries said you can use the walker for short distances here, too."

I inhale through the fear squeezing me.

"The nurse will be back soon to give you pain meds. You don't have to worry, though, because I'm keeping track of everything." She taps her notepad with her pointer finger.

I notice the scrapes on my shoulder and up and down my arms. "All I remember is Eric and me having donuts and mac and cheese, then going to sleep. What happened after that?" I strain to remember, but it's like all the important stuff has dumped out.

Then I hear voices outside my room. I glance over and see a desk with nurses and doctors and other official-looking people buzzing behind it. I spy a woman in a blazer talking loudly to a girl with long dark hair in joggers that are the same happy yellow color of the shag carpet in my bedroom. Then the woman says something. I can't hear her words, but they don't seem very happy yellow.

"Eric's dad said there was some kind of explosion." Mom's voice shakes and I turn back.

"What do you mean?"

I wish she'd put down her notes and hold my hand again.

"The camper, he said something in the back exploded."

My breath catches as panic freezes me. "Is Eric okay?"

Mom nods, straightening my blanket.

"And his dad, is he okay?" I need to fill in the stuff that's missing.

She nods again.

Relief washes over the worries gripping my insides.

"They also found Casey and brought her back," she says as she opens the blinds.

I wish Casey was cuddled at the end of my hospital bed.

"They said she smells like a smoky dog but is fine,

and Eric's aunt Josie is watching her for now. Then Eric said he'd take her." She writes something down on her notepad.

"So just me?" I say, my voice low.

She stops writing. "You were the only one in the camper at the time."

My mind swims.

"How did I get out?" I search my brain again but come up with nothing.

"Eric," Mom says. "He saved you."

I close my eyes and wonder how you thank someone for saving your life. Donuts? A note?

Then I blow out a big breath. "Well, at least it's early enough in the season that I'll still be able to be with my team for the end of fall ball."

Mom's face changes.

"Don't make the worried face, Mom. Seriously. I'll do whatever the doctor says I need to do and take whatever medicine I need to fix this." I point to my body. "But there's no way I'm missing the entire baseball season."

She's quiet.

I look at my cast, my not-moving fingers, the machines, the IV, the weird bright lights, the white walls, and my heart beats in a totally not-normal way.

"Dani, the recovery for your leg is two months with the cast and then at least a month of PT, and with the nerve damage in your shoulder"—she glances at her notes again—"the time frame for that recovery can be much longer. It's just less certain." She looks back up at me. "They also want to be sure your head is okay. I forgot to mention that part earlier. You have a mild concussion."

I bite my lip.

"Mom, I can get better faster than they think, and I finally made the team. I'm not giving up now. Not for this. Not for anything." I take a deep breath. "Also, my head is fine," I say, ignoring the hazy feeling swooshing around my brain.

She pauses. "Look, I made a chart." She hands me her notepad with its color-coded chart showing each stage of my recovery.

I stare at my mother and realize how much I hate charts.

"I know this isn't what you want to hear, Dani, but baseball's going to have to wait."

My world sways.

"And really, we just need to be grateful that you're all right." She hands me the cup with ice chips again.

I don't take it. I stare at my mom, who doesn't get it. Never got it.

Gigi got that baseball wasn't just something to do on a Saturday. It wasn't a phase.

It's who I am.

It's everything.

I shake my head. "What did the doctor say?" I ask, my nerves bleeding.

"Dr. Jeffries wants to give you time to heal." Mom blinks back her tears. "He doesn't have all the answers right now."

"Exactly. He doesn't know. You don't know." I take a big breath. "But I do. I'm going to play this season."

11

The Only Truth

It's been hours in the waiting room when I see Dani's mom walking toward us. Her eyes are puffy, and she's wearing her serious face.

"How's Dani?" Mom asks in a soft voice.

"She's going to be okay," Alice says, clearing her throat as if the thing bothering her is stuck there.

I exhale and raise my face to the yellowing ceiling tiles. *Thank you, God. I'm all over that clean room and shed.*

Mom and Dad hug Alice, then turn their hugs on me.

"I'm so relieved, but it's still going to be a lot for her. The doctor said that . . ." Alice's voice trails off.

What's happening here? Everything is fine. Dani is okay.

"Dani has nerve damage in her right shoulder, a slight concussion, and a fractured right tibia." She pauses. "But she's determined and strong."

The voice in my head kicks on.

Tell her this is your fault.

Go on, tell her.

Say it!

I rock my head from side to side, hoping to turn my brain off.

Alice continues. "Thankfully she didn't sustain any burns. The doctor thinks the cabinets and door that fell on her in the explosion and likely caused the fracture and nerve damage, also somehow shielded her from the fire and most of the debris." She lets out a big breath of air. "He said she was lucky she got out of there before the fire spread to the front of the camper. But she'll need lots of physical therapy, and right now she can't use her right arm and hand."

Why does she keep doing that? Saying Dani's good, then saying something that's the opposite of good?

Mom puts her arm around Alice.

"Honestly, I'm okay," Alice says. "Grateful, really. Dani's all right."

Then she turns to me as if seeing me for the first time.

She knows this is my fault.

I look away. I don't want to talk to her. Not now.

"Thank you," she says.

For almost killing your daughter?

"You saved Dani's life." She says it like it's the only truth.

I feel sick.

If you knew the whole truth, you'd hate me.

But all I say is "I'm sorry."

Alice steps back. "Eric, it's okay."

"It's *not* okay. Dani's in here and I'm not."

And this is my fault!

"You being in the hospital with Dani wouldn't make her better." She blows her nose. "Just promise me you'll look out for her when she gets out of here."

I promise like I'm not the worst friend in the world.

Then my phone buzzes. It's a text from Dani.

U here? Come visit.

I stare at my phone. I want to see her before she finds out. Before she hates me.

But I'm scared.

I'm to blame and soon she'll know.

I can't hide from Dani.

12

A Large Troll

"Hi," Mom says, pulling her hair into a tight ponytail. "These came while you were down the hall getting imaging on your shoulder." She points to the baseball balloons in the corner of my hospital room. "They're from the team."

I roll to the right but quickly realize my mistake as the pain shoots up from my leg. I grit my teeth to dull the hurt.

It doesn't work.

Mom pauses. "The plant is from Eric's family, but he wanted me to tell you that he'll bring donuts when he visits."

"Why didn't he come back with you?"

"You were out getting those tests done."

I look at my phone. Text from Eric:

your mom said 2 come another time ☹️

I squeeze my good hand into a tight ball. "I need to start doing whatever I have to do to get out of this stupid bed and back with my team."

The space between us grows, and all I hear is the beeping machines until a nurse walks in. The nurse is round with a flat chin and kind eyes. "Name's Reed. Nurse Reed to you, sugar," he says with a hint of Southern accent. "On a scale of one to ten, ten being the worst, how is your pain?"

"Seven."

He frowns sympathetically. "Tell me what's hurting."

Everything.

"My right leg is throbbing. It feels like a large troll is sitting on my shoulder. And my right fingers feel tingly and numb."

"I'm sorry you're in pain." He lays his hand on the metal rail on the side of my bed, and I notice the sparkly ring on his pinky. "The throbbing is from the fracture, the troll is from the swelling, and the numbness and tingling are because of the nerve damage. I promise, rest, physical therapy, and the medicine will help with all of it." He pauses. "How's your head?"

"Fuzzy."

He nods. "That's the concussion. Rest up and I'll check on you again a little later."

"Um, before you go, do you know anything more about baseball? As in me playing it?"

Nurse Reed shoots a glance at my mom, who looks at me and tilts her head like *I already told you*.

Before Nurse Reed can answer, I gesture with my good arm to my broken body. "I know not right now. Obviously." I roll my eyes. "But, like, when? Because I made the baseball team, and I need to get back to practice. I mean, it was a huge deal. Before me, the team was all boys."

Nurse Reed waves his hands in the air like he's celebrating. "I knew there was something special about you." He winks.

"See, you get it," I say, hope sneaking in.

"I do, sugar. That's exactly the attitude that's going to get you better, too. As for timing, all I know is the most important thing you can do right now is focus on healing your body."

What about my heart?

"Before I leave, do you need to use the bathroom?" he asks.

My embarrassment fills the room.

"Nothing to be ashamed of. This is a hospital. Plus, happy to ask Nurse Bell to step in. She's a love." He winks. "This is what we do. I already put an extender on your toilet." He points to the bathroom, where I see a toilet with metal handles over the regular-person toilet. "But honestly, you might be better off with a bedpan for now."

I close my eyes and wish with every ounce of me that this was not my life.

Bedpan or old-person toilet?

Are these seriously my choices?

I inhale a shaky breath, open my eyes, and say, "I'm all set. Thanks."

"Okay. Ring if you need me." He points to the call button by my bed. "Otherwise, I'll be back in a bit to give you meds and see how you're doing." Nurse Reed heads out the door, probably to help some other patient go to the bathroom.

I try to readjust my pillow and wince as the pain pings across my shoulder.

Mom comes over. I wait for her to reach for my hand.

But she doesn't take it.

I slip my hand back under the sheet like her distance doesn't sting.

"Don't worry, Dani. I can help with everything. Showering. Getting dressed. Going to the bathroom. Whatever you need." She smiles like having my mother assist me with these things is somehow less horrifying. "But now I'm desperate for a decent cup of coffee. I'm going to see if I can get something drinkable from the cafeteria. Want anything?"

I shake my head, because what I want, you can't get in a cafeteria.

Mom straightens my blanket and leaves.

I see the girl from earlier in the hallway, the one with long black hair and happy yellow pants. She walks past my door and stops. Then I hear footsteps shuffling back. She peeks in.

"Hey," she says, running her hand over her long braid. "I know you."

My brain is a mix of confusion and pain.

"You go to Mapleville Middle School, right? Sixth grade? Well, I mean, you would be going. Um, will be." The girl steps into my room like we're friends. "When you get out of this place."

I try to nod, but the medicine makes me feel wobbly, so I'm not sure if my head is actually moving.

"I'm Meadow." She gives me a half wave. "My little sister Millie is down the hall."

I stare at her and realize I do recognize her. I mean, not like we're friends. Meadow Riggs is one of those super popular kids at school. She nodded at me once but was surrounded by lots of kids, so maybe the nod wasn't really at me.

"Dani," I say, waving with the hand that can do that.

She holds out a red Jell-O. "Want it?" She moves closer to my bed. "Trust me, this is the best flavor. Stay away from orange. It tastes like throw-up."

I smile.

"You're that baseball girl, right?"

A zip of happiness shoots across my heart. "Yep, that's me," I say.

13

Worst Friend in the World

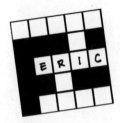

I wake up to Casey licking my face. Aunt Josie dropped her off when we got home last night. I pet her behind her soft ears and hope she won't hate me for hurting her human when the truth comes out.

Last night Dani texted that she ran into Meadow Riggs at the hospital and that she seemed nice. Which was confusing, since Meadow's one of those kids from school who says mean stuff like it's funny. But it's not. I texted back a lot of question marks and a what-are-you-talking-about emoji. Then my brain wouldn't stop spinning. It's as if the moment the world got quiet, a million tangled thoughts kicked in. Eventually I gave up and watched funny cat videos with Casey until my mind shut down.

I roll over and grab the crossword from my nightstand, glad today isn't one of those days when Zoe's standing at the edge of my bed waiting for me to wake up. I can't handle her big, trusting eyes staring at me. The ones that believe I'm not a terrible person.

Clue for 9 across: "Differences of opinion," and the third letter is F. Nothing. For 35 down: "Rancid." Nothing. For 33 across: "Artificial caves." Nothing.

Knock. Knock.

I throw on the gray sweatpants living in a pile on the floor in the middle of my room. "Come in."

It's Mom. "How are you?"

I shrug, my eyes fixed on the superhero mobile that Dani and I made in second grade.

Mom leans in. "You know, what you did for Dani was incredibly brave."

I shake my head.

"Eric, you ran into a fire to save your best friend." Her eyes are wet. "That's bravery." She pauses and puts her hand on top of mine. "But it was also reckless."

I look up, hoping I'm not in trouble for something else.

"You could have been seriously hurt, or worse," she says.

I sigh. "But it was Dani. It wasn't like there was a

choice. I had to do it." I sit back on my bed and tuck under my wool blanket.

"I understand that. Your infinite willingness to help the people you care most about is one of the many reasons I love you. But in the future, I need you to think about you, too." Her breath's a mix of coffee and mint.

I nod.

"I know this is a lot to process. You can talk to me." She waits for me to share.

My words are ready.

I open my mouth to tell her everything. The whole truth. But as the sentences form in my brain, I wonder if she'll hate me. Then I wonder if moms can do that.

I close my mouth and bite the hangnail dangling from my thumb.

We sit like this for a while, the only sounds coming from my gerbils, spinning on their wheel. Then she says, "I love you, infinity," as she gets up and walks out of my room.

Her words hang like a deadweight around my neck.

I look around and start cleaning. We have a deal, me and God.

Most of the stuff in here reminds me of Dani. The red-and-white foam finger that says RED SOX RULE. The clown statue I won at the Barnstable County Fair that she convinced me was cool and not creepy at all. And the purple stain on the carpet from the time we tried to dye wooden dreidels with beets and blueberries for the temple Hanuk-kah party.

I grab the dirty clothes from the floor and stick them in the wicker hamper at the end of my bed. I put the photo of me, Dani, and Casey at Chapin Beach on my nightstand. I took it when Casey was just a puppy. It was right before she peed on my new flip-flops.

Then I hear Dad's voice traveling up from the kitchen. He's on the phone with Alice. I shove some clean socks in a drawer and head downstairs.

"Eric!" Zoe shouts as she runs in from the other room, throwing her arms around me.

"Hey, Peanut." I scoop her up and know that even she'll hate me when she learns the accident was all my fault. Dani's one of her favorite people. For Zoe's last birthday, Dani got them matching GIRLS ROCK T-shirts.

Dad hangs up the phone and sips his coffee. "Alice asked if we've heard anything on the cause of the explosion."

I stop breathing.

"Have you?"

Please say no. I'm not ready for everyone to know.

"Nothing yet. The fire investigation is ongoing," Dad says. "But hopefully we'll have some answers later today when we go back to the campsite."

Please, no answers yet.

I see my reflection in the glass cabinet.

You're the worst friend in the world.

Dad shakes his head. "I've gone over everything we did that morning, and I can't think of a single explanation as to why it happened. We weren't using portable heaters or electric blankets. The camper wasn't new but didn't have many miles on it, and the stove was off."

My body freezes.

The stove was supposed to be off, because I was supposed to have turned it off. But did I?

There's a loud knock at the door.

"Hello." It's our neighbor and friend Jade. She's wearing a PEACE, LOVE AND SOFTBALL cap. My dad looks like he's expecting her. Jade Zhang is an investigative reporter for a podcast he loves called *Let's Talk Dollars and Sense*. She plays on the temple's 0-8 softball team with Dad and some other grown-ups from the neighborhood. Jade hugs my father and pats my shoulder. "Glad you're both all right." Then she runs her hands through her short, straight hair. It's black with a streak of blue in the front. "I stopped by Alice's, but no one answered. How's Dani?"

And together Jade and I listen as my dad unknowingly tells the story of how I ruined my best friend's life.

14

You and Me

I sit in my hospital bed and stare at the white ceiling. I miss my yellow room. I miss Casey. I miss baseball. I miss it all. It's only been a day since the explosion that changed everything, but it feels like forever. Time in the hospital is less days and nights and more long stretches of boredom and pain interrupted by doctors and nurses floating in at all hours to change bandages, look at the beeping machine, and give me medicine.

I shift to the right to ask Mom to hand me my water and a sharp pain reminds me that my body doesn't like that direction. I close my eyes, and with my good hand I trace the buttons on my Chris Sale jersey to distract from the jabbing sensation. The jersey fits easily over my sore, swollen shoulder and is way better than wearing a hospital gown. Only downside is Mom had to help me put it on, since I can't button or do anything with my right hand.

"Hello, Dani."

I open my eyes and there's a good-looking guy with dreadlocks standing in front of me. He smiles. "I'm Waylan. I'll be your physical therapist."

"Hi," I say.

Mom walks over to the bed, introduces herself, and pulls out a lined yellow pad.

I cringe as she shoots off her long list of questions, but Waylan listens patiently while she speed-reads down the paper. Then he smiles and I notice his chocolate-brown eyes.

"I'm sorry this happened to your daughter and understand there's a lot of uncertainty right now." Waylan steps closer to my mom and, in a gentle voice, says, "The best way for me to help Dani is to evaluate her movement, get her to sit up and, eventually, out of bed."

A sliver of hope slides in.

Waylan is my ticket back to baseball.

"I'm ready when you are," I say. "Just tell me what I need to do to get better fast. I made the baseball team."

"Congratulations," he says.

"The all-boys baseball team." I smile.

"Impressive."

I hold my breath. "So, what's the plan? How do I get out of here and back to my team?"

"One step at a time. Our goal right now is simple: I want to have you sit up and see how your body moves."

"Me too." I point to my leg and shoulder. "But how, exactly?" I ask softly.

"With my help." He lays his phone on my tray table. "Before we do anything, do you like music?"

I nod.

"Great. I think everything's better with music, and this is one of my favorite playlists. It's 'The Best of the '70s.' Tell me what you think."

Waylan hums and sings while we see what my body can and can't do. I learn that I can't lift my right arm to my shoulder or above my head, and my right hand is completely useless. He gives me putty to squeeze and a yellow band to wrap over my fingers to try to get them moving. Each color band is a different weight. Yellow is the easiest. I need to get to green.

He shows me how to use the button on the side of my hospital bed to slowly raise myself up to sit. Which feels kind of pathetic. I mean, I never thought I'd need help sitting.

But if I'm going to get out of here, he tells me, I need to sit up, stand, and be able to use the pathetic walker to get to the bathroom.

When we reach the last song on the playlist, he says, "You did great. You'll be sore after this, but that's normal."

"Not sure any of this is normal," I mumble.

Waylan nods. "It'll get better, Dani. I promise you."

"It has to." I glance at my mom, who's staring at her phone. "But if I'm being honest, it kind of feels like there's a giant mountain between *this* and better."

He pulls up a chair, leans on his knees, and looks at me. "You're not climbing alone, my friend."

I try to smile.

"We're strong, you and me. I promise that I'll be here for you every step of the way."

There's something about his words that makes me believe him.

I stare at the wall behind him and remember the feel of my fingers wrapped around the baseball, the smell of the grass on the field, and the sound of the ball landing in my glove.

Then I see Meadow in the hall with her sister. She waves and says she'll stop by my room later.

I wave back, surprised that someone like Meadow Riggs wants to hang out with someone like me.

"Aw, I love it!" Waylan says, full of sunshine. "My favorite people know each other."

I glance down the hall again. Meadow's little sister tucks her bandaged hand into the giant pocket of her sweatshirt.

And I wish I had a pocket large enough to hide all the things that are hurting me.

15
Slivers and Bits

I stretch my legs across the leather couch in the family room, trying to ignore Mom's not-so-quiet finger tapping as I read and reread Dani's text.

Where are you? Im bored and you promised 🍩⛪

Dani's text has been sitting on my phone for over an hour. But there's an asteroid-sized part of me that's terrified to visit. I can't pretend with Dani. She was the first one who knew something was wrong last year, even before she read all the mean stuff Leo plastered online about me. She saw my face after English class and said, "Spill it." After I showed her the meme that Leo had posted, she shared her sour gummies and made a list of all the reasons why Leo was a jerk, and another list of things that would make me feel better, which included eating more gummies.

I'm not sure I'm ready for her to know the whole truth. It's been two days since the accident, and for now, I'm hiding. And praying this wasn't my fault.

Can't today. Going to Cape with my dad to get the stuff from the campsite that wasn't totally destroyed. Will visit soon. 👍 *And promise there will be* 🍩🍩🍩

I bite the hangnail that refuses to stop being annoying. It bleeds and I wipe it against my shorts.

"Wait here." Mom gets up from her reading chair and returns with one of Zoe's princess Band-Aids.

"Seriously?" I ask.

"These are the only ones we have."

I wrap Princess Jasmine tightly around my thumb, wishing I could fix everything with a Band-Aid.

"Time to go," Dad says, walking into the room.

Dad was going to go by himself, but I begged to join him. I'm hoping I'll find something in the burnt mess that tells me this wasn't my fault.

We head out. His classic rock music fills the car.

After we've been on the road for a while, I fidget, shove my hands under my butt, and ask, "Do you think Dani hates me?"

"Why would she hate you?" Dad says, turning down "Free Fallin' " by Tom Petty.

Because I ruined her life.

I shrug and stare out the window at the red Prius in the next lane.

Just tell him.

"Eric, you pulled Dani out of a burning camper," Dad says, like that's the only thing that matters.

Do I get credit for saving her life if I'm the one who put her in danger?

The conversation dies a natural death when Dad starts singing along to his favorite Petty song. I open my crossword app. For 5 across: "7 letter word for 'hurl'." I type: THROWUP.

It takes about an hour to get to the bridge. The Cape Cod Canal stares up at me. I roll down my window and wait for the feeling to come. The one I love. The one that smells like salty air and feels like fishing and cannonballs off the dock. But it doesn't.

After about thirty more minutes we pull in to the campground. As we drive up the dirt road to our campsite, I see that the ground's covered with smoky dust, scorched gravel, and metal debris. Dad parks and we get out.

I see the charred camper, and my mind winds back to the loud boom.

Smoke. Heat. Fire.

The odors swim under my nose. I sway and everything blurs.

I clutch my stomach and heave until even my breakfast disappears.

Dad kneels by my side.

My forehead is wet and sweaty.

"It's okay to wait in the car," he says.

"I'm coming with you. Just give me a minute." I want to do this with him. I have to. I need answers. So after a few minutes, he hands me a water bottle. I rinse my mouth and spit, take a long drink, and stand up.

We walk to the camper office and are met by a short man with silver hair whose stale breath spills onto my face as he explains what's been going on.

I leave Dad to listen to the boring details of what happens next and head back to the campsite. The fried camper is surrounded by burnt books and melted kitchen things. There are scraps of blue from the sleeping bags, and I step over what I think are pieces of our fishing rods. It's like everything is here, but not really. It's slivers and bits and burnt pieces.

Then I see it out of the corner of my eye. Wedged under what had been the bathroom door and something else less definable. I'm not sure if I'm allowed to, but I pick it up and slide it under my jacket. It's Betty, Dani's favorite glove. Shoved against my body, it feels like a vise squeezing my guilt.

I walk over to my dad, who's pacing the site and talking to himself.

"Just wish I knew how this happened," he says, as if the answers are hidden in the seared dirt beneath his feet.

We pick through the rest of the rubble. Charred pots, burnt books, and a melted mattress. As I walk around the camper, I notice a mug on its side. I reach for the clay cup and realize it's one of the mugs I put the mac and cheese in. I drop the mug and throw up again. When my stomach's hollow, I know there's nothing here that's going to tell me this wasn't my fault.

When we leave, Dad thanks the manager and asks about the investigation. He directs us to the fire department.

"Let's drive over and see if they have any new information," Dad says.

My body tightens.

The fire station's only a few blocks away. When we pull in and park, I recognize the fire trucks from the accident and don't move.

"You coming?" Dad asks.

"No. I'm going to hang here. Not feeling great." I don't want to wait in the car, but there's no way I'm walking into that fire station so they can tell me how I caused the accident that could have killed my best friend.

My jaw hurts. I unclench my teeth, but that does nothing for my stomach. I stare at Dani's baseball glove lying by my feet, open my crossword app, and pray there's no news on the cause of the fire.

Finish half the puzzle.

No Dad.

He knows. He definitely knows.

They're probably telling him right now what an idiot-terrible-worst-ever son he has.

Click. The driver's-side door opens, and it feels like a train barreling full speed into my life.

I don't look at my dad's face.

"Eric, you should have—"

Oh no. Here it comes.

"—opened the windows. It's hot as a skillet in here." He gets in the car and puts down all the windows. "No news yet." Then he turns on Jade's podcast and we head home.

Another thank-you-God moment. Maybe I'm getting better at this praying thing.

"What took so long?"

"The fire investigator in charge of the case wasn't at his desk. When he finally got back, he said they should have more information soon."

The word *soon* grips my chest.

"Dad, um, what do you think happened?" I ask, staring out the window.

He shrugs. "I have no idea."

"What if someone forgot to do something? Could that be a thing that, you know, um, caused the fire?" I cough and think about all the words I'm not saying.

"Maybe," he says. "Depends what they forgot to do, I suppose."

My guilt pulls at me.

I look at my dad, then back out the window, then at Dad again.

The spit pools at the top of my throat.

"What if *I* forgot to do something?" I ask, staring at the floor, too afraid to see my father's face.

"What are you talking about?" Dad turns right out of the parking lot.

My heart races.

"I mean, what if I forgot to do something and the accident was my fault?"

"How could it be your fault?"

I should stop talking. I don't know anything for sure.

Jade Zhang's voice is all I hear for the next long minute.

Then Dad asks again, "Eric, how could it be your fault?"

My worries snake to the surface. "Dad, we had mac and cheese." I pause and say it again, slower and louder. "We. Had. Mac. And. Cheese." I wait, hoping he understands what I'm trying to say without actually having to say the words out loud.

He doesn't react.

Then my words tumble out and there's nothing I can do to stop myself. My guilt needs a place to go. "I made the mac and cheese. I was the last one to use the stove."

He turns off the podcast.

Silence.

I look over at him and see the pieces beginning to connect.

"What if I forgot to shut off the burner on the stove?" I swallow hard.

Dad sighs loudly.

"Well, did you?" he asks as if the only reason I don't know if I turned off the stove is because I haven't asked myself that one stupid question.

"I think so," I say quietly. "But I can't remember. I mean, I'm pretty sure, but I don't know. Maybe." I trip over every syllable.

"How can you not know if you turned off the stove? It's not like I'm asking if you took out the trash." The sincerity slips from his voice.

I wish I'd said nothing. But it's too late now.

I sink farther into my seat as all my past forgetful mess-ups spill between us.

When we get home, music is playing in the kitchen and there's a bowl of spaghetti and meatballs sitting in the middle of the table. Casey trails Mom as she takes the garlic bread out of the oven, and I want to freeze this moment. The moment before both of my parents think I'm the worst son ever.

Mom brings the bread over, and I reroute around my father. It's just the three of us. Zoe's with Aunt Josie.

"Did you talk to Alice? How's Dani?" I sit down next to my mom.

She puts her hand on top of mine. "The same. Stable."

I dump my head in my hands. "*Stable* is such a stupid word," I snap.

"Eric, watch your tone, please," Dad says, tugging on his beard. This is his tell. He does it when he's upset.

"That's not what you really want to say, Dad, is it?" I stare at my father, daring him to share my secret. "Why don't you just tell her?"

He looks at me. "Eric, we don't have to do this right now."

"What are you talking about?" Mom turns to Dad, to me, back to Dad.

The pressure of the last few days erupts inside me.

I stand up and the words tumble out. "It was my fault! The fire. The explosion. Dani. Everything!"

Relief mixes with self-hatred.

Mom searches my dad's face for a sign that this isn't as bad as it sounds, but there is none.

"You always say how I forget everything," I continue. "Well, this time I think I forgot to shut off the stove!"

A shocked look flashes across my mom's face. She quickly replaces it with her I-love-you-to-infinity face.

I pace around the table. "I mean, maybe I turned off the stove, but I don't remember. Maybe. But what if I forgot? I don't know. What if *I* did this?" I pause and sit back down. "Mom, I'm scared."

She rests her hand on mine. "It's going to be okay. We'll handle whatever this is together."

I hide my face in my hands. "I'm sorry."

I leave my meatballs, garlic bread, and parents and head to my room. The guilt trails me like a shadow. I close my door, but I can still hear my parents talking.

"Do you think we should say something to Alice?" Mom asks.

Please don't tell her.

"Not yet."

"Agreed," she says. "The truth is, we're not even certain what happened. Eric could have just spun himself into a worried frenzy for nothing."

True.

"Maybe, but you know how forgetful he is." Dad's words echo up the stairs and land in the middle of my room.

I sink onto the floor, and my body deflates.

16

Trust Me

I wake up from a nap, and for one glorious moment, I forget.

In my mind I'm heading to the field to pitch before school, like I do every day.

But then I open my eyes to the bright lights and remember.

I'm not pitching.

I'm lying in a stupid hospital bed with my mom watching over me from her corner chair.

Tomorrow's the first day of sixth grade. The first fall ball practice. And I'm stuck in here attempting to use a walker to get to the bathroom, trying and failing to raise my arm and move my fingers, and squeezing my quads to strengthen them.

Life is happening without me.

I take a giant breath in and remember what Waylan said. I've got this. I'm not climbing alone.

I texted Eric to visit, but he said he can't but he'll be here tomorrow.

I texted back a sad face and tried to ignore the pain bouncing across my body.

Then I hear the familiar sound of the Red Sox game coming from somewhere outside my room. Fans are cheering like everything's normal.

But nothing's normal.

Earlier today I met Gretchen, the occupational therapist, who showed me how to grip a fork with fat foam around it to make it easier to hold. Spoiler: I still couldn't do it. She also gave me a reacher—a metal stick with a claw thing on the end. It's like a longer version of the one in the arcades that Eric and I used to play to win cute stuffed animals. Just a lot less fun.

I press the giant white clicker attached to my bed to put the game on the TV in my room. I want to flood my world with baseball.

The game ends with a Red Sox win, 9–4. When I turn it off, the silence is deafening. I look around and know I need to do something. I can't just evaporate in this hospital.

"Mom, will you roll me down the hall?"

She pops up. "Sure. Where to?"

I don't want to tell her in case my plan doesn't work. "Just down the hall."

We buzz the nurse to help me stand and get into the wheelchair. It hurts, which feels equal parts embarrassing and frustrating.

Once I'm in the wheelchair, Mom rolls me past the kid in the room next to me who sneezes really loudly and the person two doors down who likes jazz. I sometimes hear their music floating down the hall.

I notice the door to room 401 is open and ask Mom to slow down. As we pass the room, I see Meadow sitting on the end of her sister's bed.

Hoping this isn't a dumb idea, I motion for Mom to stop, and knock.

Meadow turns toward the door and waves.

"Hi," I say.

Meadow puts her finger to her lips and points to her sleeping sister. She and her mom come out of their room, which looks exactly like mine except for the GET WELL sign and rainbow hearts all over the walls.

The moms talk and I turn to Meadow. "Nurse Reed told me about a sunroom at the end of the hall. Want to go?" I ask.

She nods.

Mom gives me instructions on what I can and can't do

from another list she's got on her phone, and tells me that she'll meet me back in our room.

Meadow pushes me to the end of the hall, and the sun pours into the space. It's less a room and more a corner with a few chairs, an ugly rust carpet, and a painting of the dunes along the beach. But there are no beeping machines. Just the bag with clear fluid that Mom hooked onto the back of my wheelchair. So immediately I love it.

Meadow drags over one of the chrome chairs. "You're lucky your mom gives you space."

"I guess. She spends a lot of time making lists for me and doing marketing for the company she works for. They make pickles and relish and stuff like that."

"That's cool. Not the lists, but you must get lots of free pickles."

I nod and try to ignore the tingling in my right hand.

"My mom's glued to my little sister," Meadow continues. "I mean, she barely even notices I'm in the room."

"Oh," I say. Mostly because I don't think the space between me and Mom is lucky, but also because I feel sad for Meadow.

"Whatever. It's fine. She's just being a mom, I get it." She slides back her headband. "Anyway, isn't Waylan totally hot?"

I laugh. Which feels good. And nod, because she's right.

"How did your physical therapy go?"

"Torture. But it's what I need to get back to baseball, and he promised it wouldn't always be like this."

"He's right," she says. "It gets better."

"How do you know?" I ask.

She looks at her sneakers with the pink stars, then back at me. "He's really helped my little sister."

"Why's she here?"

She bites her lip. "Her hand got slammed in the car door. It crushed some of her fingers."

"Wow, that's scary. How did it happen?"

She pauses, then says, "My older brother, Remi, did it."

"Yikes."

"It was a total freak accident. He thought she was getting out of the car on the other side." She pauses. "It wasn't his fault. I mean, it was, but it wasn't."

"Is she mad?"

"She knows he didn't do it on purpose."

Then she moves closer to me, and I smell the strawberry candy floating around her mouth. "But just between us, he feels horrible." She shows me a photo of her sister's hand. The top parts of three of her fingers are totally crushed by the nails. Her eyes fill with tears. "And then it got infected, which is why she's still in the hospital." She takes a deep breath. "It *was* his fault. So I'd get it if she hates him forever."

"Totally," I say. "I mean, she's stuck with messed-up fingers whether it was an accident or not."

"What about you? Are you mad?" she asks.

"Burning mad." I inhale all the stale hospital air around me. "I'm mad I worked so hard to make the team and I'm not out there pitching. I'm mad I can't walk or shower or do anything on my own. I'm mad I'm stuck here. I'm mad the right side of my body hurts all the time. And I'm mad that my mom and Dr. Jeffries and Nurse Reed keep talking like I'm not going to play baseball this season."

The words pour out of me. I'm surprised how easy it is to talk to Meadow. I guess I thought I would have told Eric all this stuff, but he's not here and there's no emoji for all the things I'm mad about.

"You'll definitely be out there," Meadow says.

"Right?" I stare at Meadow, thankful she gets it and surprised she gets me.

"Totally. Girl power. You didn't fight to be on the boys' team just to fade away."

"Exactly!"

"You know, tomorrow's the first day of school," Meadow says.

"Yep. Mad about that, too. I hate being in the hospital." My voice grows louder. "This is my third day here, and I want to do something crazy, but I can't even do that. I mean, look at me!"

Meadow's quiet for a while. Then says, "I have an idea. Do you trust me?"

I slowly nod.

She leaves the room for a minute and comes back with scissors.

"What are those for?" I ask.

"You said you wanted to do something crazy," she says. "And I just saw a video where someone did this with a friend and it was amazing and got, like, so many views."

I think she just called me her friend.

She pulls out her phone. "So let's make a TikTok."

"Okay," I say nervously, not sure where this is headed and why she needs scissors.

"We can call it Say It or Do It."

"Isn't that just Truth or Dare?"

Meadow smiles. "I guess, but we can't be TikTok famous with something that's been done a bazillion times before." She winks, then hits Record. "Hey, it's Meadow and Dani, straight from Harlow Hospital."

She looks at me and smiles, and for the first time since getting to this stupid place, I feel something good.

"Time to liven things up around here. We're starting things off with a Do It," Meadow says. "Dani, are you ready?"

"Wait, why am I first?" My eyes widen.

"Because you said you wanted to do something crazy."

She's right, I did say that.

"So, do you?" she asks me. Then she turns back to the camera. "Or was that just something you said?"

My stomach drops. This feels like a trick question, but

I don't want to say that with the camera staring at me, so I don't respond.

Then Meadow props the phone on the windowsill, grabs the scissors, and turns toward me. "Eyes closed, Dani. You don't get to see it until I'm done."

I shut my eyes and hope this wasn't a huge mistake.

17

A Dozen Donuts and a Nap

"Morning," Zoe sings, hopping onto the edge of my bed. "Look! I lost a tooth." She smiles big, revealing a new gap in her teeth.

"Way to go, Peanut."

"And it's the first day of school!" She twirls in her Sleeping Beauty dress and then picks up Dani's glove. "Why are you sleeping with this? It's not even cuddly."

"I'm not sleeping with it. I threw it at the end of my bed and then fell asleep."

"So you did sleep with it." She dances around my room with the glove.

"No, I fell asleep with it *on* my bed. There's a difference. Anyway, it's Dani's. I'm keeping it for her."

She stops. "Until when?"

"Not sure." I have no idea when I'm giving it to Dani. *If* I'm giving it to Dani. "I'll take the glove and meet you in the kitchen in a few." I roll out of bed and drag my desk chair across the wooden floor to the closet. I climb onto the chair and set Dani's glove next to the unfinished super-hero comic I started writing when Dani left for baseball camp this summer.

My phone pings, a new text from Dani. I assume it's about my visit after school today. I'm still scared—petrified, really—but I know that I can't hide from her forever. So my new plan: tell her the whole truth and pray she doesn't hate me.

But the text isn't about my visit. It's a TikTok link. I click on it and watch. It's called Say It or Do It, and it's of Meadow Riggs cutting Dani's hair. Then I watch again. I'm not sure if I'm more shocked that Dani's doing this with Meadow or that Dani doesn't really look like Dani. Her hair is still brown and wavy, but now it hangs above her shoulders and swings when she moves her head.

I show the video to Casey, who looks equally confused. I watch it a few more times and text back a thumbs-up. I mean, her hair looks good, I guess, if I ignore the Meadow part. It just doesn't look like Dani.

I get dressed and go downstairs.

I pass on Dad's waffles, wave to Zoe, who's watching Big Bird sing the recycling song, endure a don't-worry-I'll-love-you-even-if-you're-a-terrible-person look from Mom, and head out to my first day of sixth grade.

Alone.

The air's misty and it feels strange walking to school by myself. When Dani and I were little, we walked with our moms. Then last year when we started middle school, we walked by ourselves after enduring our parents' safety speech. This morning there's no speech. And no Dani.

When I get to school, I scan for any sign of Leo and exhale when I don't see him. But as I walk through the halls, my stomach feels like a vat of flies is having a dance party. Kids stare and point. Everyone seems to know about the explosion.

Kiki Brown taps my shoulder. "How's Dani?" she asks. I spin around to answer, but the words are trapped.

As I turn the corner, I hear someone say, "Hey, man, heard about Dani." It's Matías, another sixth grader from my neighborhood. "Also heard that you, like, totally saved her. Very cool."

"Thanks," I say, hoping my face isn't as red as it feels.

I tell Matías I'll catch up with him later at the Speak Out! meeting after school and run smack into Coach Levi. "Hey, Eric. Please tell Dani that the team is thinking of her."

I nod.

"I'm glad you're both okay. And what you did was quite brave."

My cheeks feel even hotter now. "Um, thanks," I say and head to Ms. Brattle's science class.

As I slip into a seat in the back row, my guilt finds me. People think I did something great. I mean, I guess I did. Which is cool. But I'm pretty sure I also did something not so great. Which is less cool.

Ms. Brattle begins her introduction to sixth-grade science, and I realize I forgot to bring in my hypothesis for this experiment we're doing. She emailed the class two weeks ago, introducing herself and giving us the assignment. I stare out the window and think about all the other things I may have forgotten. Then I think about Dani saying she wanted to go to sleep that night at the campsite. Dani lying on the floor of the trailer, pinned under the kitchen cabinets.

Somewhere during my train of thought, class ends. I wipe my eyes with the back of my hand, grab my books, and go to English.

I don't pay much attention in the rest of my classes. I feel like I need a dozen glazed donuts and a nap. All I can think about is the accident and my stupid, forgetful brain.

But in the halls around me, everyone's lives seem normal. Unfazed. It's weird. Carlton can't stop talking about the Red Sox win. Willow wants to know if AJ likes her or Bethany. And Max shaved his head at band camp. I don't care about any of that stuff.

All I want is for things to be the way they were.

Before.

The.

Accident.

The bell rings. School's over and the first meeting for Speak Out! is about to start. I sit down and Rachel walks in. She looks like goddess meets mermaid—minus the fins— and smells like honeysuckle.

She smiles at a person who is not me, and I pray she can't tell I'm a horrible human just by looking at me.

Ms. Suarez shares how glad she is to see everyone and how much she looks forward to working together this school year. She rambles on about submission ideas, cell phone numbers, contact information, deadlines, and causes to work on. Then she tosses our names into a gray fedora and all the categories into the plastic bowl on her desk.

"Okay, people to my right. Pick a name from the hat and a topic from the bowl. You'll be working in pairs. We need your ideas in the next few weeks. Any thoughts or questions, just let me know."

Quinn picks Jason and climate change, Omar gets Andrew and politics, Callie gets Keegan and education. Next, it's Rachel's turn. She pushes her long blond hair behind her ear, stretches her fingers with the purple nail polish into the hat, looks at the slip of paper in her hand, and says, "Eric, we're partners." She smiles.

I swallow and pray there are no hives splattered on my neck.

Her hand goes into the bowl. "And we'll be focusing on safety."

When the meeting ends, Rachel finds me at my locker, and all intelligible thoughts leach out of my brain.

"H-hi," I stammer.

Not the best start.

"Hey," she says. "I'm sorry about Dani. How's she doing?"

"She's had better days." My mind spins, but nothing more coherent surfaces, so I shove my hands into my pockets and stop talking.

Behind her I see Leo coming down the hall. My insides tighten, but I don't move. I'm hoping he'll ignore me and keep walking. But he doesn't. He stops at my locker and slams the door shut.

Fear worms across my chest.

"Heard about Dani," he says, sticking his face in mine. His breath smells like roadkill. "What did you do, man?"

I dodge the spit flying out of his mouth. It feels like all the air is seeping out of my lungs. I say, "You're an idiot." Not clever but accurate.

"Whoa!" Leo says. "I was just joking. Aren't you supposed to be, like, her friend or something?"

My body folds in.

"Knock it off, Leo," Rachel says. "Did you know that Eric saved Dani? He pulled her out of a camper that was on fire. He's a total hero." Rachel shoos Leo away like an annoying gnat.

I'm the furthest thing from a hero.

Rachel turns back to me. "Ignore him."

I nod, like every fiber in my body isn't looking for a place to hide.

"You walking home?" she asks. Rachel lives a few streets over from me.

"Yeah," I say.

"Want company?" Rachel says.

It takes me a minute to realize that *she* wants to walk home with *me*. Talk to *me*. "Sure," I say, trying to sound casual. Like I haven't been wishing for this since fourth grade.

"Nice shirt." She points to my Iron Man T-shirt.

"Thanks." I turn around and show her the picture of Tony Stark in all his gear on the back.

"Cool."

"About what Leo said." I crack my knuckles, exhale too loudly, and stare at the concrete sidewalk.

"He's an idiot."

I nod and hide the truth.

She walks over to the stone wall in front of the house with the angel statue in the yard and hops up. I follow.

"So what causes do you think we should work on?" She twirls a strand of hair around her finger.

"Maybe we could do something on the new Iron Man movie." I smile.

"It has to be about safety stuff," she says.

"Well, Iron Man has to be careful. Those jetpacks are dangerous."

She laughs. "Maybe," she says. "Or we could do something about all the potholes on the hardtop at school. Principal James talked about being careful out there in his morning announcements."

"Yeah, that's true. That's when he mentioned the band uniforms."

"They're really nice." Rachel's dad donated the new band uniforms. She swings her legs back and forth against the stone wall. I notice the silver polish with white dots on her toenails, and my mind fogs.

"Let's each make a list of three things we could work on and then swap," she says.

"Sounds good."

"Is that today's crossword puzzle?" She points to the paper sticking out of the front pocket of my backpack.

"Yeah. It's the one from *The Clippings*. My parents are old school. Still get the newspaper delivered."

We fill in most of the puzzle with her purple pen.

Her hand grazes mine, and I decide that purple is my new favorite color.

A while later we leave the wall. She turns down her street, and I head home.

When I walk into my house, Mom's standing at the door, waiting for me. "How was your first day?"

"Okay."

"Do you like your classes?"

"They're fine." I open the refrigerator and grab a yogurt.

"And the club. How was that?"

"Also fine." I leave out the parts about Leo and Rachel.

"Glad it went well." She pauses and picks up her jacket and purse. "Why don't you finish your snack, put your bag in your room, and then we can head out."

"Where are we going?" I ask, my brain still stuck on all things purple.

"To the hospital to visit Dani. Remember?"

My body freezes.

I nod as mounds of nerves trample my happy honey-suckle feeling. Because as much as I want to see Dani, I'm not ready for her to know the truth.

18

All the Things I Hate

Mom's writing something on her notepad while I lie in my hospital bed, staring into the small, rhinestone-studded handheld mirror. I tilt my head left and then right. My new hair sways with me.

Yesterday, after chopping off my hair, Meadow said, "Looks great. Kind of like rocker chic meets movie star. At least, that's what I was going for. Do you like it?" She sounded hesitant, which was weird. I mean, why was *she* nervous? She has all her hair.

I nodded. "Yeah. I think so. Thanks."

"You're totally rockin' it, and I can fix that one part where it came out a little uneven in the back if you want,"

Meadow said, braiding her still-long hair. That's when Mom walked over. "Wow! Love the new look," she said.

I was kind of surprised she liked it and relieved she wasn't mad. Mom's not great with change, especially since Gigi died. She hasn't even packed up Gigi's room yet. Which kind of works for me. Because some days I like to just sit on Gigi's honey-colored bedspread with Casey. Like everything's the same. Even if I know in my heart that it isn't.

"Right, Ms. Meyer?" Meadow said. "Dani looks bold." Then she left my room to help her sister with her physical therapy exercises.

I realize Meadow's right. I do look different. But I don't think it's bold. I definitely don't feel bold.

I feel angry . . . scared . . . frustrated.

I stare at the mirror again. My once-long hair now hits my chin.

I'm not sure I even know this person looking back at me.

I inhale and exhale and inhale and exhale, trying to find my peace, my place, myself. My leg throbs and I wonder if it's possible to lose who you are in pain and frustration. I look in the mirror again.

I don't want to lose me.

I want to fight.

For everything.

My phone buzzes. Eric's almost here. He gave a thumbs-up to the TikTok of the new me with my new hair. No mention of Meadow. Which I'm kind of happy about. I know he thinks she's a jerk, but the truth is, people change. She's not that person anymore.

I'm thinking about that when the door creaks open. It's Eric and his parents.

I wave with my good hand, and Mom walks over to them, something I haven't fully mastered yet. But, as of an hour ago, I can at least sit up, stand, and take a few steps with the walker. So that's something.

Eric smiles awkwardly, looks away, then back at me, and away again. Which seems weird. But then he shows me the box of promised donuts, which seems much less weird.

Beep. Beep.

The monitors grunt. Eric inches closer, sits in the chair next to my bed, and puts his hand on his bobbing knee.

"Hey," I say, turning down the bright light above my head.

"Hi," he says. "Nice hair."

I smile at the Princess Jasmine Band-Aid on his hand and am glad he's here.

"We're going to leave you guys alone," my mom tells us as the parents head to the cafeteria.

As soon as the last grown-up is out the door, Eric inches his chair closer and says, "I'm sorry."

"For what?" I ask, confused. "You didn't do anything."

He cracks his knuckles.

I take a sip of water. My mouth feels desert dry. "I wish none of us had been in the camper, then I wouldn't be in this dumb place either."

"Me too," he says. Then points to my cast and holds up a Sharpie. "Can I sign it?"

I nod. "Just be gentle."

He carefully writes his name in big black letters down my cast. Then he nervously scans the room and stares at the floor and the ceiling and out the window.

"Why are you acting so bizarre?" I say, my hurt showing.

"I'm not. I mean, maybe I am. I've just never seen you lying in a hospital bed all hooked up to stuff, that's all." Eric turns his eyes away from me and talks to the blank television screen.

I hate this.

"I'm sorry. I didn't mean—"

I don't say anything. I just push the red button and lower the top part of my bed to hide my disappointment. I was excited to see Eric, but now I don't know. He's making everything awkward.

Eric slowly rolls his eyes back onto me, but only from the neck up. Or maybe he's just looking at the top of my head. The quiet emptiness fills the room until he blurts out, "I, um, went to school."

I raise the top of my bed a bit.

Maybe if we talk about normal stuff, it'll all feel less weird.

"How'd it go?"

"It was okay." He fidgets in his chair.

"Did you get McDermott for math? Heard he's the one to avoid." I grit my teeth, hoping it will stifle the itchiness climbing up my skin.

"Nope. I got Lamont."

"Are we in any of the same classes?"

"Homeroom with Rhodes."

As he talks, tiredness worms into every inch of my body. I yawn and try to stretch, forgetting that my right arm won't extend above my head.

"What else?" I ask, hoping to distract him from whatever not-normal thing my arm may be doing.

"Rachel's in history with me."

"Don't wear that when you have history." I point with the hand that works to his Iron Man T-shirt.

"Too late. I saw her at the club meeting and was actually wearing this very shirt." He smiles. "Everyone loves a superhero."

"Is Iron Man really a superhero, though?" I laugh.

He smiles. "Despite my shirt, she talked to me." Then he says, "Saw Coach Levi, too. He and the team were asking about you."

"Is McKinnon pitching?"

Eric shrugs. "Don't know."

"Well, even if he is, it won't be for long," I say, ignoring the pain traveling up my leg.

"I didn't think you'd be able to play again so soon," he says, picking at his Band-Aid.

My frustration simmers.

"I mean, like, this season. You know, since, um, this." He points to my broken body.

"Well, I'm not missing my chance. It took forever to make the team." I feel the despair slipping into my words. "I'm going to play."

"Yeah. Sure. I mean, um, that's great."

I look at the row of get-well cards. "I hate this. All of it," I say. In my mind I make a list of everything I hate:

white walls

the smell of vomit and alcohol and feet

my blue cast

all Jell-O

the old-person toilet

pain

my useless right hand

the stupid stuff grown-ups say

being scared

I never had a hate list before. Now I have a pretty long one.

I swallow and reroute away from the things I hate. There's something I need to say to Eric in person. I look at my friend. "Thanks for saving Casey and me."

Eric coughs.

"It's a big deal," I say. "Like, Iron Man big deal."

He doesn't say anything. Instead, he grabs a deck of cards from his neon-green backpack. The one I told him to get, so when he forgets it somewhere, it'll be easy to find.

"How about a game? I even remembered the M&M's so we can ante up," Eric says.

I nod. His aunt Josie taught us how to play Gin Rummy one Saturday night after we ate her world's greatest lasagna.

Eric gives us each a pile of M&M's, deals us both ten cards facedown, then puts the rest of the deck in a pile on the tray table, turning over the top card.

I stare at my ten cards, slide them into a stack, and grab them with my left hand.

Did it!

But they're out of order

I blow out a breath.

I need to organize them. I can't though. I literally can't. My right hand is tingling and numb and completely useless.

I add this to the list of things I hate.

I look up at Eric, who's focused on his own cards.

Okay, come on. I can do this.

Using my one good hand, I slide the jack of spades out of my stack and onto the bed. Then I carefully slide the other two jacks onto the bed as well, moving the three cards into their own little pile.

But when I put the pile back into my hand while holding the other cards, the jack of clubs shifts. I try to use my thumb to hold it in place, but it falls.

Then they all fall.

Tumbling out of my left hand.

Sliding off the bed.

Onto the white tile floor.

Eric's face goes pale. "We don't have to do this," he says, bending down to pick up the scattered cards.

I look out the window. I'm trying hard to be me, but that person is moving further and further away.

Eric wriggles in his chair, his knee at full speed. He gathers the cards, shoves the deck back in his backpack, and grabs his fidget spinner. "We can just hang out. There's, um, something I need to tell you anyway."

"Okay," I say.

"Before I say it, though, you need to know it was a total accident."

"What are you talking about?" I ask.

"And that I'm really sorry."

"Why do you keep saying you're sorry? You're not making any sense."

Then I hear our parents coming down the hall. Mom's voice is loud.

I turn to my best friend. "Eric, what's going on?"

He stares at his black high-tops and says, "This was all my fault."

19

Anchor Between Us

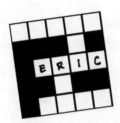

Alice barges into the hospital room with eyes that know the truth. "Eric, I think you should leave."

"Wait," Dani says. "I need to understand what happened."

Dad drapes his arm over my shoulder. "It's important to remember that we know nothing for sure." Mom nods.

Dani turns to me.

I squeeze my hands into two tight balls. "I don't remember if I turned off the stove after I made the mac and cheese."

I hear Dani mad-breathing.

"And maybe that's what started the fire. So, I, um, could be the reason you're stuck in this stupid place."

There it is. My full confession, dropped like an anchor between us.

Disbelief spreads across Dani's face. Most of me feels like the worst person in the world. But there's a small part that's relieved to have told her.

No more lies.

No more secrets.

She uses the button on the side of the bed to raise herself. A low groan of pain escapes her lips. I move to help her, but Dani holds out her good hand. "Don't." She pauses. "How could you do this to me?"

"I didn't *mean* to."

"That's true. Even if this happened the way Eric thinks it might have, it wasn't on purpose," Mom says.

Dani ignores her. "Eric, you're supposed to be my best friend."

"It was an accident," I say.

She stares at me. "But that doesn't change this." She nods toward her bandaged leg and swollen shoulder.

"I'm sorry."

"For what?" Her voice shakes. "Making the mac and cheese when I told you I didn't want any? Forgetting to turn off the stove? Or not telling me about it?"

Alice stands next to Dani's hospital bed.

"I'm sorry for all of it," I say. But I'm pretty sure there are no words big enough to fix this.

A nurse I haven't met yet comes in. "Hello, Dani," she says. "So nice that you have company, but I'm going to need your visitors to step outside for a moment so I can change your bandage."

"They were just leaving," Dani says.

She hates me.

"I'm really sorry," I say again.

She doesn't look at me.

I hate me.

As we exit the hospital, the smell of disinfectant sticks to my Iron Man T-shirt. The car ride home feels hollow. Mom's voice interrupts my guilt spiral with things that are supposed to make me feel better:

We don't know anything yet for sure.

Dani will come around.

People make mistakes.

It was an accident.

But as I stare out the window, all I see is the wave of sadness that crashed between Dani and me when I told her my truth.

I bite the inside of my cheek and wish she was mad instead. Even really mad. Because mad feels temporary. But sad feels like something that sticks.

When we get home, I throw myself onto my bed. I hold

my phone and think about texting Dani but have no idea what else to say. Instead I check for any updated information on the fire investigation, hoping maybe I'm not the worst person in the world. But there's nothing new.

Frustration pulls at me.

My phone buzzes.

Maybe it's Dani.

Maybe she forgives me.

But it's not. It's Rachel. And as much as I want her to text me, my excitement is stuck behind a mountain of guilt.

Did you finish the crossword? Got your 3 ideas?

I read it again.

I shove my guilt down deep and try to respond like I'm not a horrible person. I wish Dani was here or didn't hate me. She'd know what I should say so I don't sound stupid.

I pace around my room and think about how to respond. I type and read and delete, certain it sounds totally dumb. Then type again. Delete. Pace. Type one more time. *Crossword almost done. My ideas: 1—Iron Man movie (still believe jetpack safety counts) 2—Hot dog eating contests (stay with me here, I love hot dogs but there's no way eating so many so fast isn't dangerous)* 🌭 *3—Innocent stuff that's dangerous like magnets. Heard kids try to eat them. Gross and unsafe*

Read it over and hit Send.

I dump the contents of my backpack onto my desk. My homework spills out with my shame.

I hate that I'm the most forgetful person in the entire world.

I hate that my brain can't hold the stuff it's supposed to remember.

And I hate that everyone knows it.

I pick up my Spanish homework. I need to teach the class in Spanish how to do a crossword puzzle, but I can't focus. I rub the fur between Casey's ears. My mind wanders back to Dani.

I shake my head and tell myself to concentrate. I think about crosswords and Aunt Josie, the crossword master, which leads to me thinking about Charles, her cat, then about other cats, and then watching cute cat videos. There's one with a hairless cat like Charles, which brings me back to Aunt Josie.

Then the day in the hospital parking lot.

Which takes me to being the worst friend ever.

Then to crosswords and Spanish.

Then back to the worst friend ever.

I close my eyes and wish I had a brain that didn't ping like a pinball machine. I pet Casey some more, hoping that might help.

I grab my crossword puzzle. I have only a few more to fill in. Clue for 21 across: "The epitome of slipperiness." Oh. EEL. Perfect. On to 24 down: "Of the highest class." ELITE. Two left. For 45 across: "Bone in forearm." I twist and bend my arm. No idea. Not even the start of an idea. Then my phone buzzes.

It's a text from Rachel with her ideas: *1—Hardtop potholes—I mean, how can kids play basketball with holes all over the court? 2—Iron Man jetpacks (almost convinced this qualifies) 3—Not enough lifeguards at the beach* 😎 🏖️

My brain's clouded with guilt and cats and crosswords, so I just text: *Let's go with 1 or 2 or hot dogs.*

Then I follow the navy zigzags on the carpet and grab my crossword.

Need a word for a bone in forearm. Send.

How many letters

Does she know more than one?

Four. Send.

ULNA

It fits. Totally impressed.

I finish the crossword and my mind floats back to Dani and the accident. I don't want to think about it.

But not thinking about it feels like I'm hiding all over again.

20

Parade of Ants

My phone buzzes. It's Eric: *Sorry Sorry Sorry*

I don't respond. This is his sixth apology text since he left the hospital.

Then another buzz: *I can fix this. I promise.*

My heart hurts in ways I didn't know were possible. I toss my phone on the bed.

My leg itches. It feels like a parade of ants marching across my skin. I so badly want to ask Mom for a ruler to shove under my cast. But I already know I can't do anything but breathe deep, meditate, and try to think about something else. That's what Waylan said this morning at

PT. Which seems totally unfair, since the only thing crowding my brain is how itchy my leg is.

And baseball.

Waylan and I talked about that, too. I promised him I was going to keep working hard. Get it done. Get back out there.

"That's what I like to hear, my friend," he said as he counted my quad squeezes and then helped me stand and use the walker so my body doesn't weaken and shrivel up. "That attitude is what's helping you get stronger, Dani. That's why you can already sit up, stand, and almost walk to the bathroom with the walker. That's the winning mentality that will get you back to baseball."

I smiled.

Then he hesitated.

And in that beat of nothing, worry crept in.

My world slowed.

"But it's not likely going to be this season."

The lights felt hot on my skin.

"You don't know that. Dr. Jeffries doesn't know that." My voice was loud. "You just said I was doing great."

Mom looked up from her phone. "Honey, all of us just want you to be realistic about your recovery," she said. "It's going to be past the end of baseball season before you—"

"You don't get it!" I turned off the lights above me, but my body still felt like it was burning from the inside. "You never got it. You don't even like baseball."

"That's not true. I love you and don't want you to be

disappointed. That's all. I just want you to understand what's possible."

"But anything's possible! That's the point. I didn't make the boys' team by accepting the limits and stupid things people kept telling me."

"Honey, please don't raise your voice," Mom said.

"It's okay," Waylan said. "I understand."

They kept talking, but I'd stopped listening. I thought I could do this if I just worked hard. Then the cards fell, and now I'm not sure of anything.

Knock. Knock.

My mind flips back to now. It's Coach Levi. "Okay to come in?" he says from the other side of the door.

Mom looks at me and I nod.

"Of course! We're happy to see you," she says.

"How's one of my favorite Mapleville players doing?" Coach says.

My heart dips.

"Dani, pitching or not, you're still part of the team." He takes a Mapleville baseball hat from behind his back. "That's the thing about us, we're family." He hands me the hat, and I notice it's signed by all my teammates.

My insides churn. "Thanks, Coach." I slide the cap over my short hair with my left hand.

He stays for a bit. We talk mostly about the Red Sox, and then Mom walks him to the elevator. I look in the handheld mirror at my team hat, and a sliver of pride slips in. Then the machine that monitors everything beeps, and my pride's replaced with frustration.

I hate this place.

I'm adding beeping monitors to the top of my hate list when I see Meadow and a boy who looks a little older than Meadow with greasy black hair.

Meadow waves and comes in my room, and the boy heads down the hall.

"Hi," she says. "I told you I'd still visit."

I smile. Her sister was discharged yesterday, but Meadow promised she'd stop by whenever Millie came back for PT with Waylan.

"I'm happy you're here," I say, trying to ignore the pain *tap tap tapping* my shoulder. "And, great news, Dr. Jeffries said if I can walk all the way to the bathroom with the walker tomorrow, I can get out of here, too."

She hugs me.

"Who was that with you?" I ask her.

"Oh, that's Remi, my brother," Meadow says softly. "I told him where they keep the red Jell-O." Meadow sits in the chair next to the bed. "Busy?"

I grimace. Busy feels like a nonexistent state here.

She moves the jacket from the back of the chair and sits down. It's Eric's. Of course he left it.

"How's your sister?" I ask, taking off my team cap.

She shrugs. "Okay, I guess."

"It's nice that you spend so much time with her." I look

around my empty room, wondering how long Mom will be talking to Coach. "Kind of wish I had a sister."

"Well, now you have me."

"Thanks," I say, smiling.

"How'd it go with your BFF?" she asks, extending her long fingers and laying them across her lap. I notice the blue polish on her ring finger.

Can I trust her?

I look at her a little longer. "Not good." Then I share what happened. The truth. The whole truth.

"Whoa. So not really your BFF anymore." She hands me a red Jell-O. I hold it with the only hand that works, and she pulls the lid off. Then I put it in my lap and grab the spoon with my left hand to eat it. Feels backward. Like I'm wearing shoes on the wrong feet.

"I don't know. Right now I'm just sad. I mean, how could he have done this to me? If he'd just listened to me that night, none of this would've happened. I told him I didn't want the stupid mac and cheese. I told him I wanted to go to sleep." I grab the yellow putty with my left hand, put it in the palm of my right, and try to squeeze like Waylan showed me. But my right hand doesn't move. Nothing happens except fear sliding into cracks of doubt.

"Seems pretty selfish," Meadow says, slurping her Jell-O. "You know, like he did what *he* wanted and now you're stuck here and he's out there living his best life."

"I didn't think about it like that."

I try to squeeze the putty again, but still nothing.

"Well, maybe you should. Because he didn't just do what *he* wanted. He went and lied about it." She tosses the empty Jell-O cup in the trash. "Even worse."

Anger ricochets across my body. Maybe Meadow's right. Maybe Eric didn't care what I wanted, then he hid the truth. A tightness pinches my chest.

"I didn't want to say anything before because you were so psyched to see him," Meadow continues. "But I know Eric. I mean, we're not friends, but yeah, not surprised he'd do something like this. My cousin Leo's told me stories about him. They're kind of hysterical."

"Wait, you and Leo are cousins?"

She nods and my stomach splinters.

"Yeah, it's weird. Most people don't even know we're related. I think it's because we hang with different groups at school and basically just see each other at family stuff."

She pauses. "Either way, let's forget about BFFs who don't act like BFFs. Let's forget about baseball."

Let's forget that you're cousins with the enemy.

She eyes me. "Let's do something fun."

"Like what?" I look around my hospital room. "Not sure how many fun choices I have here." I pause. "And I'm not shaving my head."

She laughs. "Okay, shaving your head is out. What about another TikTok?"

"Of what?"

"Us. I mean, you're stuck in here while everyone else is living their life." She pauses. "No offense."

I nod because it's true. I mean, kids from the neighborhood have reached out and told me they love my new hair. Juanita from baseball camp keeps texting me funny animal GIFs, and the baseball team sent stuff. But everyone's life is normal. Not some bad version of normal.

Meadow continues: "We need to do something before you die of boredom."

She's right. But . . . "Why are you doing this?" I ask. I need to know. Especially now.

"It's what friends do," she says, popping a piece of strawberry gum in her mouth.

I'm friends with Meadow Riggs.

"Besides, I'm here anyway with my sister. Might as well do something fun while I'm waiting around for her to finish PT. Right?"

"Okay. Let's do it." I smile and a little happiness slides in. I'm grateful to have a friend like Meadow. A friend who cares about me. A friend who doesn't lie. Even if she's related to Leo.

Meadow pulls out her phone. She takes a small tube from her pocket, dabs strawberry gloss across her lips, and offers me some. I do the same, even though I've never even worn Chapstick.

She gives me a thumbs-up, and I feel good in a totally new and different way.

She scoots next to me the way friends do, props the phone on a stack of pillows, and hits Record. "Meadow and Dani here. Bringing you another episode of Say It or Do It, straight from Harlow Hospital."

I wave with my good hand.

Meadow talks and laughs like we're hanging at her house eating pizza. Not sitting in a hospital eating Jell-O.

"Okay, I'll go first this time." I turn to Meadow: "Say It or Do It?"

She smiles at the camera. "Say it."

"Who are you crushing on?" I hesitate, kind of stunned that I asked Meadow Riggs this question.

She taps her chin with her long nails, raises one eyebrow, and says, "Wouldn't you like to know?" Then she dishes how Aditi likes Pat, Greg likes Shannon, and Rome just wants to sing "Memory" for the school musical, *Cats*. She turns to me and says, "Say It or Do It?"

"Wait, you didn't answer."

She smiles. "No one's really interested in me. But I know our fans want to hear from you."

The camera stares at me, so I go with it. "Okay, since we're not shaving my head, I'm picking Say It."

"Remember, you wanted it," she says with a wink. Then she says, "Is Eric Stein responsible for the accident that landed you in this hospital?"

My stomach drops and I don't respond.

"Well, seems this one's got her stumped. Stay tuned, time will tell." Then she signs off.

I turn toward her. "Why did you do that?" My voice comes out higher than I wanted it to.

"What?"

"Ask me that about Eric?"

"He messed up big time. You practically said it yourself, you're sad and he's selfish. So if we're really talking truth, why not share it all?"

21

Sinking Feeling

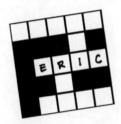

It's only morning and I already hate today. I saw Dani's latest TikTok video. I tried calling, texting, but nothing. Just a whole lot of silence.

Then Mom told me at breakfast that Dani's getting out of the hospital later this afternoon, and there's some kind of welcome-home party thing. Dad said they'd patched things up with Alice and it's important that we all attend together.

But I can't even think about how messed up that is right now. All I can think about is that Dani told Meadow everything. Then just sat there and let her basically tell everyone that the accident was my fault.

I mean, maybe it was and maybe I deserve for everyone to know I'm the worst friend ever. But I never thought Dani would do this to me. I thought it would make a difference to her that it was a mistake. That she'd forgive me. That she'd keep it between us.

But now the entire school knows, and that's a whole other bucket of unfair.

I eat waffles, share bites with Casey, toss my gray hoodie on over my newest Avengers tee, and walk to school. In the hall I wave to some kid I know from math last year. He says, "Whoa. Thought you and Dani were friends." I tuck my hand back into my pocket and pick up the pace. Another kid I don't know says in a way-too-loud voice, "That's messed up, man."

I pull on my hood, stare at the tiles on the floor, and try pretending he's wrong. Try ignoring the words ripping at my heart.

But it's hard. Because no matter how annoyed I am with Dani or how mad I am at Meadow, they're not totally wrong.

This *is* my fault.

In history I slide into a seat next to Rachel. I cross my fingers, hoping she hasn't seen the latest Say It or Do It, but by the look in her eyes, I can tell she has. "That's gotta sting," she says, offering me pity and a piece of gum.

I take the stick of spearmint. "Just so you know, there's more to this. It's not what you think. I mean, I just don't know. I can't remember what happened. That's all." I stop talking, because I'm not sure my words are making anything better.

"I forget stuff, too," she says, tucking her hair behind her ear. "And I wouldn't want someone blabbing about it to the whole school."

"Thanks," I say.

I don't eat lunch in the cafeteria, because I don't want to bump into Leo or Meadow. Instead, I find an empty spot in the room where we met for Speak Out!, open my brown paper bag lunch, and eat my glazed donut first. Something Mom recommends when you have lots of complicated feelings bouncing around your body.

I'm relieved when the school day ends, until I spy Leo standing, arms crossed, in front of my locker.

Nerves worm across my chest.

God, if you're there, a little help would be great.

"You need to move," I say, hoping I sound bigger, stronger, and more confident than I feel.

"What are you going to do about it, burn down the hall?" His voice is loud and echoes through the circle of kids starting to crowd around.

I see the staring eyes, and my insides twist. "I need to get my stuff," I say.

He doesn't budge. "Well, guess you're going to have to get through me, then."

My knees wobble as beads of sweat slip down my back.

"All good here?" It's Coach Levi, dispersing the circle of gawkers with a wave and a "Get home."

"Sure," Leo says. "We're just joking around. Right?" He shoulder-checks me, laughs, and walks away.

"You okay?" Coach asks.

I nod, grab my stuff, and head home, my brain crowded with embarrassment.

When I walk into the kitchen, Mom's standing there with her no-kidding, I've-got-important-things-to-tell-you face.

My worry spikes. I stop in the doorway for a few stand-still seconds. A sinking feeling stabs my insides.

God, I'm not sure I can take another bad thing right now.

"How was your day?" Mom asks, her voice low.

I'm too nervous to answer.

"Why are you here? I mean, home? Why are you home? You said you'd be working late?"

She walks toward me.

What did I forget to do this time?

I step back.

"What's going on?" I drop my backpack onto the kitchen floor and stare at the geranium that's drooped in the pot on the windowsill. The one I didn't remember to water.

Mom touches my shoulder.

Don't.

> *Do.*

> > *That.*

She leans in and says in a voice coated with love, "We got a copy of the fire investigative report while you were at school."

My stomach tightens.

I can barely breathe.

I'm scared of the truth. Scared to know if I really am the most horrible, forgetful, worst friend in the whole world.

My hands shake. I stuff them in my pockets and try to breathe like a normal person.

Then Mom says, "The accident wasn't your fault."

My worry slams to a screeching stop.

Mom hugs my frozen body. "It wasn't your fault."

She gives me the report. I regain my senses and scan the paper until I get to the part where it lists the cause of the explosion. I hold my breath and read: "Cause of explosion: defective lithium-ion battery in remote-control car."

I read it again and start pacing around the room.

"What does this mean?"

"It means the explosion wasn't your fault," Mom says. Her voice is steady, certain, unwavering. "There was something wrong with the battery in the remote-control car."

"The one Dad got me that looked like our camper?"

She nods.

I stop moving. "What if the explosion was because of me *and* the defect thing? Like, I brought the stupid thing on our trip."

She walks over and puts her arm around me. "Eric, it

wasn't your fault. The stove was off. The toy car was defective. This had nothing to do with you. They investigated and found it was the defect alone that caused the fire."

My body uncoils.

I didn't do this. I'm not the worst friend ever.

"But *how* did it happen?" I ask.

Mom looks at the report again. "It says something about the battery overheating."

"We never even turned the car on. All I did was plug it in." I pace around the kitchen table.

"They think it caught fire while it was charging, and then the fire spread to the rug or bedding in the back of the camper, then must have ignited something like a gas line or some such, which caused the explosion that shattered the back windows. From there it just kept going."

The windows were closed. Dani was cold.

My head's pounding. "Do you mean it was broken when Dad bought it?"

"I guess." She rests her hand on mine. "For now, the important thing is that you're not to blame."

Maybe she's right. Maybe all that matters is that it's not my fault.

I exhale. And finally let go of the guilt.

This report will fix everything.

22

The Jell-O World

It's been four long days in the hospital. I can't wait to get away from beeping machines and sick people and the smell of alcohol mixed with vomit and feet. This morning with Waylan, I sat, stood, and walked to the bathroom with the walker. Then Dr. Jeffries said that I was ready to be discharged.

Meadow FaceTimed me earlier today: "Your hair still looks great, and when you get out of there this afternoon, I promise to bring you red Jell-O so you feel right at home."

"Very funny," I said. "After this, I'm never eating Jell-O again."

I look over at Mom, who's making lists for my medication, my physical therapy, when I went to the bathroom (I'm not even kidding), and the people I need to write thank-you notes to. Then she lifts her head from her notepad. "I forgot to tell you. I invited some friends and family over as a kind of a welcome-home party. I included Eric and his family. I worked things out with Mr. and Mrs. Stein. Apologized, really. It was an accident, after all," she says, like this is the only thing that matters.

"Oh." I inhale the knot wedged in the back of my throat. I don't want things to be weird with Eric when I get home. Not today. But I also don't want to make her feel bad, so I just say, "Fine."

And the truth is, home feels kind of terrifying for other reasons that are taking over my brain right now. I mean, I'm ready to say good-bye to this place, but what if I get those sharp pains in my leg in the middle of the night? It's not like I can push a button on my bed and a nurse will magically appear and take care of me. What if the medication makes me woozy? Like the time Nurse Reed played *Crossword King* with me until the throw-up feeling went away.

I know Mom will help, but in her practical, let's-make-a-chart-for-everything way. Not in the hold-my-hand way.

And what if I puke in front of all the people coming to this party?

Mom smiles at me and packs my toothbrush and pajamas. I smile back and wish she'd stop doing that stuff and just sit with me and talk, the way we used to.

I glance over. Her gray hair is in a clip on top of her head. Kind of how I wore mine before Meadow cut it off. I run my hands through my short hair and remember when Gigi lost all her hair. Well, I guess she didn't actually *lose* all of it. Some fell out and some Mom buzzed off. Every afternoon Gigi and I had iced tea with lemon and talked about baseball. And every afternoon she had less and less hair. I never said anything, but it was hard not to notice the empty splotches on her head. Then one day, she sat down at the kitchen table and told Mom to buzz it off. All of it.

I'd hoped by now that memory would have disappeared or been replaced with something else. Anything else. But it's still there. The buzz of the razor like a wasp in my ear. Gigi's dyed-blond curls tumbling to the floor. Me looking out the window above the sink, wrapped in my fuzzy yellow fleece. The moment the buzzing stopped and my grandmother was bald.

Mom puts her notepad in her tote and the rest of the stuff in the duffel. I hold tight to my lucky coin, though. I mean, after everything that happened, I feel like it kind of saved me. And for now, it's still mine, at least until Eric wants it back.

We haven't spoken since our fight or the TikTok video. Which is weird. Him coming to the welcome-home thing, also weird. But maybe weirder if he didn't come. I mean, his whole family will be here, plus, he has my dog.

I hate that everything's so annoyingly confusing.

Another thing to add to my hate list.

"Okay. It's time," Mom says. She locks the wheels of the wheelchair and helps me into it. The doctor said I'm stuck in this thing mostly for school and when I'm out in the world, until I get the strength and feeling back in my right hand. But at home I should use the walker. Then, when I get stronger, I get forearm crutches. Then regular walking. Then baseball.

Mom may have lists.

But I have a plan.

I stare at the gray clouds so Mom can't see the pain spreading across my body as I use my left arm to lower myself into the chair. Waylan and I practiced this move, but no matter how many times I do it, it still feels like daggers stabbing my leg.

"I'm thankful you're coming home, Dani," Mom says, extending the footrest for my right leg and hanging my backpack over the arm of the wheelchair. She rests her hand on my good shoulder. It sits there for just a few seconds, but to me it's everything.

"Yeah, me too," I say.

As we pull out of the hospital parking lot, I watch through the car window as the clump of medical buildings turns into apartment complexes with statues of important people and circles of dirt filled with flowers, which morphs into brick houses with green yards and pet dogs playing Frisbee.

When we pass the Ander Arboretum, I hold my breath. Our street is the next one on the left, and I don't know if I'm ready.

We turn onto Willow Lane, and I spy a sign above my front door that says WELCOME HOME, DANI! I recognize my mom's handwriting. She's the only one whose *w*'s look like a cross between an ocean wave and a flying bird.

Mom lifts the wheelchair out of the trunk of the car. It takes me a lifetime to inch my way out of the back seat.

Come on. Just do it how Waylan showed you.

I reach with my good arm, clench my teeth, and slide into the wheelchair.

Then Mom navigates the chair over the ridges and roots jutting out from the driveway, which is a lot harder than pushing it along the hospital's smooth tile floor.

She eases me up the ramp that she said Eric's dad finished late last night and into the house. I look around, taking in all the changes. The big circle rug with the tassels in the family room is gone so I can glide my walker and wheelchair across the wood floor. The ugly couch with the matching ugly chairs are sadly still here, but pushed back so I don't bang into them. And the very fragile glass penguin statue is now on a bookshelf—I guess so I don't bump into it and break it.

"Welcome home, Dani," Mom says, a bouquet of happy-face balloons behind her. She's smiling but her neck is blotchy red.

The house smells like a bakery. There's a table full of blueberry muffins, scones, double chocolate chip cookies, and some kind of strawberry pie.

"Thanks, Mom," I say, taking a bite of a blueberry muffin. Then I see her bringing the walker out. "Can I use it?"

She nods and helps me out of the wheelchair. I slowly step into the walker, putting my left hand on the grip and resting my right forearm flat on the piece attached to the top since I still can't grip with that hand. I take a few steps. They're small and they hurt, but I'm doing it.

Mom's phone rings. She looks at the number and sighs. "I bet it's another lawyer. You know, the ones from those television commercials. They keep calling," she says. "Give me one minute."

She takes the call in the kitchen, and I shuffle turtle-speed down the hallway. I bump into the wall only a few times before I pass the bathroom and see a chair in the shower and one of those old-person extenders on the toilet. I honestly can't believe this is my life. Last night in the hospital, when Mom was helping me sponge myself clean—as if that wasn't embarrassing enough—I realized I can't even wash my own hair or the entire left side of my body without assistance. I also learned that actually showering means I need to cover my entire cast in Saran wrap so it doesn't get wet. Another thing I'll need help doing.

I close my eyes and try to center myself. One thing at a time. That's what Waylan says. So for now I'm going to focus on the best blueberry muffins ever and being home.

Knock. Knock.

I slowly head back into the family room and see Coach Levi's head peeking through the front door. "Okay to come in? I know I'm early, but duty calls." He tugs on the brim of his Mapleville cap.

I nod.

"I have a gift from the team. They heard you like donuts." He holds out a box filled with chocolate, glazed, jelly, powder, Boston cream, and vanilla with rainbow sprinkles.

I can't really grab it and hold the walker, so he puts the box on the table with all of Mom's baked goods. "That's nice. I'm certain they'll taste a lot better than hospital food."

He laughs. "So how are you?"

I'm not sure how to answer, so I go with "Better than I was. Not as good as I'm going to be."

"Sounds fair."

"But don't worry, Coach, I'll be back out there with you and the team soon. I promise."

He smiles. "That's what I was hoping you'd say."

Joy shimmies in.

"Because I wanted to know if you'd be our third-base coach."

Wait, what?

I stare at Coach Levi.

And that's when I know I'm not pitching this season.

23

Couch of Awkwardness

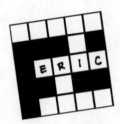

Casey speeds ahead of me, passes Coach Levi, who's just leaving Dani's house, noses the open front door, and darts toward Dani.

"I missed you," Dani says, leaning over the walker, trying to hug her dog with one arm.

Then she looks up at me and I notice that her eyes are red.

"You okay?" I ask.

"Yep, fine," she says in a way that doesn't sound fine. "Thanks for bringing Casey back."

I shove my hands in my pockets, hoping to slow down my brain, but the words burst out of me anyway. "Did you see the report?"

This is it.

No more guilt.

No more feeling bad.

Just me and Dani, like before.

Dani shakes her head.

"Turns out I'm not as forgetful as I thought." I bow. "The cause of the fire was *not me*," I say triumphantly.

"Are you sure?" She asks like she can't imagine the fire being caused by anything *but* me.

I nod and ignore the hurt rising from her doubt. "One hundred percent. It was in the report. None of this was my fault."

"Well, if it wasn't you, then what was it?"

I take a deep breath. I thought she'd be happier about it. "You're not going to believe this. It was the remote-control car. You know, the one that looked like our mini camper. Something about the battery in it overheated and caused the fire." I take a glazed donut from the table and sit on the ugly flowered couch.

Dani sighs.

Why isn't she excited that we know what happened? Relieved it wasn't me? Happy we can go back to the way things were?

"Weird. We never even used it." She puts her left hand on the arm of the couch and slowly lowers herself.

"That's the confusing part. But now that we know that none of this was my fault, Meadow can take back or fix or apologize for the stuff she said on your show."

"Yeah," Dani says. "Not sure Meadow's the kind of person who says she's sorry for a lot of things."

"Oh." I look away. "Well, then, *you* do it. Leo's been a jerk, and what Meadow said has made things worse." I put the second half of the donut in my mouth.

"Got it. Things are hard." Dani's voice is sharp.

I stare at my friend and realize she's never been on the receiving end of mean. She doesn't know how it scrapes your insides hollow and sticks to the layers of your skin.

"Look, I'm not trying to be a jerk. I know things are hard for you, obviously." I take a breath. "I'm just tired of being picked on, and you were the one who said you'd have my back about the Leo stuff." I pause. "You promised."

"I *do* have your back. But you can't possibly think being picked on by some brainless idiot is the same as what I'm dealing with?"

I fidget.

"Or the same as Coach walking in here a minute ago and telling me how happy he is that I'm recovering and excited for me to rejoin the team. And just when I think some grown-up finally understands me, he says he wants me back as the third-base coach." She pauses. "Not as the pitcher—the spot I earned and worked for—but as some useless helper."

"Dani, that stinks," I say. "And what's happening with you and what's happening with me are different. But they're both bad." I rub my fingers along the fidget spinner in my pocket. "You get that, right? I mean, you're not the only one with stuff going on."

Dani doesn't say anything as the ugly couch fills with awkwardness. Then the front door opens, people file in, and the conversation ends.

"Welcome home! We're so thankful you're out of the hospital," my parents say as they walk over to Dani.

Aunt Josie hands her a bunch of sunflowers. "I told the world to heal you."

"Thanks," Dani says, grabbing the yellow-and-brown flowers with her left hand.

"I missed you so much, Dani!" Zoe runs up to Dani wearing her GIRLS ROCK T-shirt and hands her the card she made last night with tiny yellow heart stickers. The parade of people just keeps coming. There are hugs, lots of thank-Gods, and someone wearing way too much cologne that smells like a dying Christmas tree. Pretty sure it's Dani's uncle Bud.

Meadow walks in and my stomach drops.

She gives Dani a red Jell-O, and they both laugh. Then she pulls a pink marker out of her bag and draws a giant heart on Dani's cast with her name under it.

I get up, grab another donut, and sit on the chair across from the couch of awkwardness. Zoe follows and hops onto my lap. "Eric has a present for you," she tells Dani.

I look at my little sister. "No, I don't."

"Yes, you do, silly. I saw it," Zoe says. Then, in a loud

whisper, "You have her baseball glove. Remember? The one you sleep with."

Meadow laughs and I feel heat spread across my cheeks.

"I don't sleep with your glove," I say to Dani.

"Yes, you do." Zoe nods and straightens her princess crown.

"No, I don't. I found it at the campsite and brought it back for you. I thought you might want it."

"Yeah, maybe," Dani says.

"Oh. Okay." I swallow my embarrassment.

My mom and dad go into the kitchen with the other grown-ups and Zoe. Meadow disappears somewhere.

"Thanks for saving Betty. I'll want it sometime." Dani pauses. "Just not yet."

"I get it."

She tilts her head. "Do you?"

"Um, yeah. You want to do a thing and you can't. Like that time I broke my arm and couldn't go to your beach birthday party because my mom was worried that my cast would get wet."

She shakes her head. "It's that times a million. You don't know what it's like to work for something. Get it. Then lose it," she says. "I mean, you've never really cared about anything. You drop in and out of different stuff all the time."

I look at her. "You make it sound like that's bad. Maybe I just like a lot of different things."

"Yeah, but the only thing I've ever cared about is baseball. Everything's easier for you."

I stare at her. "You know that's not true. Not when I was picked last for every kickball game ever. Not when Leo decided to be an all-around jerk to me. I get that being a girl who plays baseball is hard. But—"

She glares at me.

"Okay, really hard. I get it. But you did it." I stand up and speed-walk around the couch.

"You're making me dizzy," Dani says. "Sometimes I think I'm going to wake up and realize that none of this actually happened. Like, it was just a nightmare or some new reality show where they want you to believe this bad thing happened just so they can film your reaction."

"I'm sorry, Dani." I sit back down. "I'll find a way to fix this."

"I'm not something to fix." She pauses. "Well, I guess I am. But by a doctor, not you. I'm not one of your stupid club's causes."

"That's not what I meant." I trip over my words. "All I meant was—"

Before I can finish, Meadow returns and looks at me. "What are you still doing here?"

I feel itchy blotches on my neck. "The report came back. The explosion wasn't my fault. It was something messed-up with the battery in this remote-control car we had with us on the trip."

Meadow says nothing where an apology should be.

"Like, it was defective when we bought it," I add. "So you can apologize and say *that* on your show."

Meadow shrugs. "I don't care about some stupid battery. All of this"—she motions to Dani—"was still your fault."

"That's not true. The report said the fire was caused by the broken car thing."

Meadow moves between me and Dani. "If you didn't bring the stupid broken remote-control car on the camping trip, the battery wouldn't have overheated and there would have been no fire." She stares at me. "Get it now?"

I turn to Dani. "None of this was my fault. You know that, right?"

She just looks at me. "All I know is that you can't fix what happened to me with some stupid report."

24
Not Listening

Everyone but Meadow has left the welcome-home party.

"Stop worrying about Eric," Meadow says. "He's being a brat. Annoying, really."

Meadow grabs a scone and hands me the yellow rubber band from my PT bag. I loop it over the fingers on my right hand like Waylan showed me. Then I try to stretch and extend my fingers. But I can't. My brain's talking but my fingers are still not listening.

Disappointment lingers as Meadow talks.

"The report made *him* feel better. So running over here the second you got home from the hospital to say, 'Look, it wasn't my fault'—when I kind of think it still was, but that's another thing entirely—is so selfish. The report doesn't heal *you*. It doesn't make *you* feel better." She puts her plate on the table and grabs something from a bag by the door. "He needs to grow up or move on or something. It's like he's stuck in his elementary school brain."

I think about Eric. She's right. He's been the same forever.

But I'm not.

Meadow gives me a small wrapped box. "Welcome home."

"Thanks." I pull off the shiny striped paper with my left hand. "Wow." In the box is a silver bracelet with lots of empty loops. "I love it."

"This is for the person you want to be. Whoever that is."

She helps me clasp the gift around my wrist.

"Every time you figure out something new that you like, you add a charm to the loop." She dangles her wrist and it jingles. She has a matching one with lots of charms.

I stare at it and smile. A new bracelet for the new me.

When Meadow leaves, I lie on my bed and finish my physical therapy exercises. I use my left hand to raise and lower my right arm above my head. I do my shoulder shrugs and thigh squeezes. Waylan is coming to the house this week to make sure I can get in and out of bed, the car, and the bathroom.

As I slowly lift and lower my leg, I think about what

Coach Levi said. I thought he was the one grown-up who understood me. The one who believed in me.

But I don't care what he thinks.

I don't care what anyone thinks.

I'm going to play this season.

That night I make a plan. I text Coach and ask him to meet me at the baseball field this weekend.

Mom thinks it's a bad idea. She says it's too soon. "Way too soon" were her exact words. Followed by "You're not ready."

What she doesn't get is that I know I'm not ready. It's not like I'm coming out here to show him my fastball. But it doesn't matter if I'm ready. I can't wait until then.

I need to show him now that I'm strong and healing before it's too late. He's already sidelined me, thinking the only thing I can do for our team is be the third-base coach.

I need to change his mind.

So on Saturday I use the technique the OT person showed me to get dressed. Apparently my left hand needs to do much of the work to get me in and out of clothes. Elastic-waist pants are this fall's fashion must-haves, since I can't button or zip yet. And even though Mom helps, I'm exhausted by the time I get into my stupid wheelchair.

Mom pushes me past the staring eyes and the baseball kids on the next field.

Ignore them. You can do this.

When we get to the field, Mom's got her worried face on. She parks the wheelchair. "You okay?" she asks.

"Yep," I say, hiding all the reasons that's not true.

I wave to some kids I recognize, and imagine I'm walking to the mound with my team around me.

The nerves march up my spine.

You've got this.

I close my eyes and inhale the smell of fresh-cut grass.

Before all this, that smell calmed me whenever I felt anxious or out of place. And the dirt—it's weird, but I love the dirt, too. The way it crumbles and coats everything. The way it feels like home in a strange way.

I take in another breath, and my mind settles. It's happily less fuzzy than it's been since the accident. Mom says that's a sign the concussion's getting better. I think it's a sign I'm meant to be here.

Mom puts a small green bucket on the metal bench next to me in the dugout. It's filled with the baseballs from the giant red bucket that neither of us could drag to the field.

"You sure about this?" she asks in words wrapped in uncertainty.

I nod and reach into the bucket with my left hand. I grip one of the baseballs. The stitching feels good against my palm. I exhale.

"Dani, honey, maybe we should call Coach and cancel, or just reschedule." Mom interlocks her hands like she's praying.

"Mom, it's okay. I'm okay."

She slides onto the bench. "I just don't want you to get hurt."

I look at her and then at my bruised shoulder and the blue cast holding my leg together. "Seriously?"

"Okay. I don't want you to hurt yourself *more*," she says. "I want you to get better. I'm your mom. That's my job."

"I get it, but I have to try. I have to do this."

Before she can show me her list of reasons why I should cancel, I hear "Hello!" It's Coach Levi. He waves and walks across the field toward me. "I was happy to get your text. I will say, however, that it was a surprise. I wasn't expecting you'd be back out here this soon."

See, he just doesn't know I'm a fighter.

That's all I've got to show him.

"It was nice that you could meet Dani here today," Mom says. "I'll leave you to it. If you need anything, anything at all, I'll be right over there." She points to the picnic table next to the field.

"So why did you want to meet?" Coach asks, putting a handful of sunflower seeds in his mouth.

My jaw tightens. This is it.

I take the baseball from my left hand, open my right, place it in the middle.

Now squeeze.

143

But I can't.

The ball rolls off my fingers. Out of my hand. Into the dirt.

Coach picks it up. "Dani, you don't need to do this."

"No, wait. I can do it. I can. I will. Just give me a minute." Worry builds in my chest. I put my left hand into the green bucket again.

Pull out a baseball.

Put it in my right hand.

Clench my teeth and tell my brain to hold the ball, squeeze the ball, don't let go of the ball.

But my right hand isn't listening to my brain.

The ball drops.

I do it again.

The ball drops.

And again.

The ball drops.

"Dani." Coach's voice is gentle and low. "You'll get there. You will."

My eyes sting. "I just wanted to show you that I'm stronger than you think. That I'll be able to play eventually, even if it's not until the end of the season. I wanted you to believe in me again."

"I do believe in you, Dani. You just need time."

"I hate when grown-ups say that. Like time is in charge of my life. Like I don't have a say in what happens."

"Of course you have a say. You're the boss of you, and

getting better will require all of *your* hard work. But it'll also require time." He takes off his cap and scratches his head. "Healing is a marathon, not a sprint."

Someone in the other field yells, "Bottom of the fifth." I spy the kids running off the field toward the dugout.

I miss it all.

A tear rolls down my cheek and lands in the dirt I used to love.

25

Twisted Things

My brain whirls as I gaze out the window of Mom's car. I thought the report would fix everything. But it fixed nothing.

Meadow just twisted things. Said things in a way that made them sound true even if they weren't.

And Dani didn't stop her.

That's the part I don't get.

I tune out Zoe's play-by-play of her teeth cleaning at the dentist and hop on my crossword app. Then I see Zoe sticking her freshly picked boogers on her tutu.

"Okay, Peanut, that's gross," I say to my little sister.

I look toward the blue sky. *I'm not breaking my promise, God. But you've got to agree with me here.*

"Mo-o-om, Eric called me gross," Zoe whines.

"Technically that's not true. I called her fluffy tutu thing gross because it *is* gross. It has snot all over it."

"Zoe, do you need a tissue?" Mom asks.

"Nope," Zoe says, pleased with herself.

Mom hands her a tissue anyway.

By the time we pull into our driveway, Zoe's sleeping and Mom tells me to carry Ms. Boogers to her room. To avoid getting snot all over myself, I consider holding her by her feet, but I don't want to renege on my promise to be nice to my sister. So I carefully carry her, keeping the decorated tutu as far from my body as possible.

My frustration sticks to me the next day at school. It's drizzling, but I eat in the courtyard anyway to avoid Leo, who knocked my books out of my arms this morning on my way to history. Lunch is fish surprise. I don't understand why the school thinks kids want to eat any food that ends in the word *surprise*.

When the bell rings at three o'clock, I sprint to the bathroom and grab my emergency deodorant from the bottom of my backpack. Mom bought it for me last year. It kind of smells like my dad, which isn't great, but it's better than fish surprise.

I head out to find Rachel at her locker.

"Hi!" I say, realizing I need to find a way to sound less excited every time I speak to her.

"Hey."

The little swarm of freckles on her cheeks makes that hard to do.

It also makes this day exponentially better.

I give her what's left of the crossword I started this morning. She surveys the clues and leans the puzzle against her notebook. Her hand grazes mine as she quickly fills in the answers with her purple pen.

Before Rachel I hated purple.

We walk to the stone wall, then I tell her about the report and the broken-battery thing that caused the fire.

"I can't believe it," Rachel says. "They sold it like that?"

I nod and pause to get the courage to share the idea that's been swimming in my head. I know Dani says she doesn't want me to fix things. And maybe I can't fix her. Or us. But I can try to make sure this never happens again.

"You get it. Right? This is bigger than the accident that morning at the Cape."

"It's huge! But what can *we* do about it?"

She leans closer and my brain fogs. I shake my head to clear it. "I have an idea."

"What?" she asks, swinging her sandals back and forth.

"Once, Dani and I saw this story online about a guy who lost his leg when his lawn mower went crazy. He wrote to the mower company and got them to stop selling the mower. In the interview the guy said he didn't want this to happen to anyone else. What if I write to the company that made the remote-control car, tell them what happened, and get them to stop selling the broken cars so no one else gets hurt?"

"Do you think they'll care what some kid says?"

"I don't know, but I feel like I have to try."

"I get that. Let's write it at my house." Rachel grabs my hand and leads me off the wall.

At that moment I pray my hand's not sticky.

Rachel lives in a stucco Tudor with a turret. Think castle minus the moat. And when we go inside, the house is empty except for two small fluffy white dogs, who dart toward Rachel. The family room has fancy paintings of old people's faces and a television the size of my kitchen table. I think about the letter we should write while Rachel's doing something in her room. I have no idea what to say or who to send it to.

"What's the plan?" Rachel asks, sitting next to me on the sofa.

"Um."

She stares at my blank face.

Right, I'm the one with the plan.

"Let's research the company that made the car," I manage to say.

She smells like honeysuckle again.

"Do you know the company's name?" Rachel asks.

"Yeah, RCarz." Last night I poked around my dad's office. He's a filer, and I found all the information he had on the remote-control car.

We search for RCarz and their website pops up. There are lots of colorful pictures of different types of remote-control cars, but I can't tell if any of them are like ours.

I find a page with reviews. Some are good, but a few say the cars were too expensive or came with missing parts. Nothing about them exploding. But then I see "For all questions or comments about our merchandise, please contact info@RCarz.com."

Rachel says, "Okay, that's who we have to write to."

I nod and open a new message. I think about Dani and that morning and the fear that crept into every part of me. I type until I've told the story. I lean back in my chair and read aloud what I've written.

Dear RCarz,

My name's Eric Stein and I'm twelve. I'm writing about my best friend, Dani.

I pause at this part, because I'm pretty sure Dani's not my best friend anymore. I take a deep breath and continue.

Recently Dani and I were camping on Cape Cod. Dani was alone when a fire exploded in the back of the camper. I dragged her out, but she got really hurt. The fire department investigated the accident and found that the remote-control toy camper that your company made was defective. They said the lithium-ion battery overheated and started the fire.

Dani's right tibia was fractured, and she has nerve damage in her right shoulder. She can't hold things in that hand now. And the doctor doesn't really know when it will get better. Dani's right-handed, and before the accident she was an awesome pitcher. She was even going to be the first girl on the fall baseball team this year.

I need your help. I want to make sure no one else gets hurt like this again. So I'm asking that your company stops making the defective remote-control camper and that you tell stores to stop selling it also.

Thanks,
Eric Stein

I exhale and pet Milo, one of the fluffy dogs.

"It must have been awful." Rachel rests her hand on top of mine.

"It was," I say, trying not to move my hand. I nod at the letter on my computer. "Think it's ready?"

"Definitely," she says. "Send it."

I hit Send with my other hand, and we talk until I need to leave. I get up and then awkwardly pause at the door. I want to take her hand again, but I'm pretty terrible at this, so I just wave and say, "Thanks for your help."

As I walk home, I stop at the corner of Willow Lane and look up.

Please, please, please, God, let this work.

I'll even carry around my little sister and her snot-filled tutu for an entire year.

26

Used-Tos and Maybes

I see my reflection in the bedroom mirror and wonder if my nerves are showing. Then I text Meadow. I thought it'd be Eric who I'd want with me on my first day back to school, but it's not. Which feels strange. But everything feels strange. Especially since I met Coach Levi at the field last weekend. All the things I thought I knew, all the stuff I believed I could do, dropped in the dirt with the baseballs.

Now I'm left with a lot of used-tos and maybes.

When the doorbell rings, I roll to the front door. Meadow's standing there with a navy-and-yellow tote bag that says GOOD VIBES ONLY. "Thought you could use a new book bag." She hands it to me, and I hold it up.

"Looks great with your shirt," she tells me.

"Thanks," I tell her, putting it in my lap. "And for helping me today." My lips twist. "I just can't push the wheelchair and deal with my books and getting to class on my own." I sigh. "Waylan says I need to be patient. Like I have a choice."

The smell of cranberry and cinnamon floats through the archway between the family room and the kitchen as Mom takes a tray of muffins out of the oven.

"Well, at least I don't need to deal with trying to write or type with my left hand. Principal James assigned kids to share their notes with me."

"Lucky," Meadow says. "I mean, not the whole can't-use-your-right-hand thing—that obviously stinks—just that you don't need to pay attention in class."

Pretty sure I don't think anything about this is lucky, but I nod.

Mom pokes her head out of the kitchen. "Morning, Meadow," she says, like it's a normal first day back to school. Not like she's been nervously baking cranberry muffins all morning.

"Hi," Meadow says. "Don't worry, Mrs. Meyer. Dani will be fine."

"The school is supposed to call me if she needs anything." My mom wipes her flour-dusted hand across her forehead and looks at me. "Or you can call or text me."

"I will."

Meadow grabs a too-hot-to-eat muffin and takes a tiny bite. The steam escapes into the air. "These are seriously amazing."

Mom smiles.

"Great," I say, and roll toward the door. I glide down the portable wheelchair ramp. Casey follows me but we don't let her outside. "Now can we go?"

Mom drives us to school. When we get there, she says, "I'm only five minutes away if you need anything."

"I know, Mom. I'll be fine. It's just school," I say, trying to convince myself as I lower into the wheelchair.

Meadow pushes me down the sidewalk, into the building, and through the hall. I don't say anything.

"You okay?" she asks.

"I feel like an idiot. I'm horrible at steering this thing. At home I keep knocking into walls and doorframes."

"Let's hope your skills improve before you get your driver's license."

I spit out a nervous laugh and try to ignore the kids we just passed who were 100 percent staring at me. And not in the you're-a-baseball-rock-star kind of way.

Meadow waves to the next swarm of girls who walk by, wearing matching iridescent headbands. I smile and bury the worries inching across my chest. Then Meadow stops pushing me and says, "Look, don't worry. I've got you and I promise not to knock into anything."

"Thanks."

As she pushes me into homeroom, I see Eric, who's wearing his Tony Stark sweatshirt with the hole in it. His desk is behind mine. We haven't really spoken since my welcome-home party last week, and I don't want him to start talking about the stupid report that fixed nothing. I just want this to be normal. So I squeeze the arm of my wheelchair with my left hand and say, "Nice sweatshirt."

He nods.

Kids fill in around us.

I feel people staring, and my body stiffens.

Meadow locks the brakes on my wheelchair. "Wait for me here when homeroom ends, and I'll come back and pick you up."

Eric turns to me. "*I* can just take you to your next class. I mean, I'm already here."

"Nope, I'm on it," Meadow tells Eric, twirling her long hair. "I've got it all planned out. I talked to Principal James, who talked to my teachers. I have a late pass for my classes and permission to use the elevator."

Eric ignores Meadow. "You all right?" he asks me.

I see Jamal and Katrina whispering in that way that screams *We're talking about you*.

"Totally fine," I lie.

More whispers and stares.

I swallow hard, then say to Eric, "You're doing that weird thing with your face. You look like my mom."

Meadow laughs.

Other kids laugh.

Eric's cheeks turn cherry red. But now all eyes are on him, not me.

Sorry, Eric.

"I don't look like your mom," he says, trying to undo whatever's happening on his face.

"Okay," I say. "As for later, I'm good. Meadow's got me now."

27
Donuts

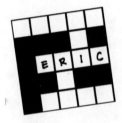

I dig out the jeans I've been wearing for the last two years. Sadly, they still fit. I shove my homework in my backpack and make a list of things to talk about at the Speak Out! meeting after school. Ms. Suarez assigns a different student to run each meeting, and today's my turn. I'm nervous. Like, flies-in-my-brain nervous. This is a first for me. Not being nervous, but leading. I'm not really the leading type. I asked Dad about it last night. He's definitely the leading type. He said I should be prepared.

So I look over my list one more time and add donuts, because I'm pretty sure donuts should be a part of every plan. Then I grab my backpack and a granola bar and leave for school. Rachel's already seated when I walk into class. We pass today's crossword from *The Clippings* between us.

We have half the puzzle completed when the bell rings. Rachel takes the crossword to work on in French but promises she'll slip it into my locker after last period.

For the rest of the afternoon, I make sure Dani's okay from a distance. I may not like this version of her, but I promised Alice that first day in the hospital that I'd look out for Dani. So after the last bell rings and I see her and Meadow get into Alice's car, I race to room 112 with lots of nerves and a dozen assorted donuts for the Speak Out! meeting. Apparently we had to switch to the seventh-grade science room for today's meeting, since the other room was reserved for a chess club tournament.

Room 112 smells like formaldehyde. Or dead things. Or both. I breathe in the smell of a glazed donut to mask the stink. I tap my foot, crack my right knuckles, then crack my left ones. While I wait for people to come, I click on the latest episode of Say It or Do It and listen for the apology that never comes. Instead, this time it's Do It for Meadow. Dani dares her to walk up to the captain of the eighth-grade football team at lunch, sit down next to him, and start eating his French fries. Meadow totally nails it, which is annoying. I wish for once she'd trip or make a fool of herself or do something that resembles what the rest of us feel like much of the time. Then Meadow and Dani spill about who's crushing on who. Turns out Joshua likes Sophie, and Rani likes Lesley, who likes basketball more than anyone in sixth grade.

I turn off my phone, exhale, and notice a poster of the anatomy of the brain tacked to the wall behind the life-sized skeleton. I wonder which part of the brain is in charge of remembering stuff.

Rachel walks in and immediately everything gets better.

"Donut?" I ask.

She grabs a powdered one and sits across from me. Her shoe touches my sneaker under the table. I'm pretty sure it's on purpose.

"Do you think I brought enough?" I ask, pointing to the almost-full bakery box.

She nods.

Halfway through my glazed donut, Matías, Greg, Omar, Vicki, Padma, Sarah, Shannon, and Destiny walk into the room. I got desperate five minutes ago and may have squeezed out a small request that this meeting goes well, making absolutely clear that all my Dani prayers still have priority. Even if Dani's being a jerk.

God, I'm not sure if it's possible to ask for too much. Or if a new prayer cancels out the ones that came before. Or if there are rules I should be following. Because if there are, that would be helpful to know.

I look around the room. Everyone's here. My heart's rapid-firing, but I stand and start by asking each group what they're working on. One by one they go around and share. Then we brainstorm storylines for coverage of the upcoming school election, talk about the different climate-change issues, and decide to host a food drive to help kids in our school and community. By the end of the meeting, the box of donuts is empty and we've nailed down many of the specific causes we're going to work on as a group.

"Hey, great job running things today," Rachel says. "Good call on the donuts. Those should be a new requirement for all our meetings."

I smile and feel happy. Like hot-dogs-at-the-Red-Sox-game happy.

In this moment I realize that maybe I *am* the leading type.

And maybe I'm more than all the things Dani thinks I'm not.

Then Rachel leans over and kisses my cheek.

Best meeting ever.

28
Just Cookies

Coach Levi meets me at the edge of the field. "Ready?"

I nod like I am, but my brain knows I'm lying.

It's been three weeks since the accident and two weeks since I met Coach at the field with the green bucket of balls. He called the other day and asked if I wanted to try again. He said, "Let's start small. Just come and hang in the dugout with the team."

I wasn't sure what to say. And while Waylan vetoed my being the third-base coach because it was "way too dangerous," he thought this plan would be good for me. I'm getting stronger and walking farther with the walker, and my hand is starting to move a little when my brain tells it to. So I told Coach I'd try.

But as I look across at the field, I think Waylan might be wrong. This place doesn't feel good for me. It feels like the past.

Coach wheels me over to the team. My stomach tightens, but I keep a smile on my face. It's not real, but no one here knows that.

The team claps. "Good to have you back," McKinnon says.

"Thanks."

Not sure I'm back, but I'm here.

My team takes the field. McKinnon throws some warm-up pitches.

Coach helps me navigate my wheelchair to the dugout. I didn't ask him to, but if I'm being honest, I'm kind of glad. I don't want to struggle here.

He parks me next to the metal bench and pats my back like I'm doing something great by just sitting. I feel hot from the inside out, and a panicky feeling squeezes my chest. I try to focus on the grass I love and shake it off.

The first batter steps up.

But it's not working. I can't swallow.

It's a fastball to the corner. Batter swings and misses.

I blink back tears.

Another pitch. Then another.

The batter strikes out.

I feel like I can't breathe.

Next batter steps up.

Not enough air.

Swings and smacks it over the second baseman. Safe at first.

I wave Coach over.

"Um." I cough and try to find my air, my breath, my voice. "I can't do this. Not yet." I pull down my baseball cap. I don't want my team to see me like this.

"It's okay, Dani. Coming here was hard, but it was also brave."

I don't feel brave. I feel pathetic.

He chews a handful of sunflower seeds.

Fake smile.

Coach helps me off the field, and my team claps for me. Which makes me feel like an even bigger failure.

I call Mom and in a few minutes she's at the school with a fresh batch of sugar cookies.

We sit in the parking lot together. No words. Just cookies.

Eventually Mom says, "Good job today."

I shake my head. "Not sure just showing up to the field is something to be proud of." From the car I see McKinnon pitching.

"I disagree. It took a lot of courage to get out there."

Someone hits a fly ball to right field.

"Well, it feels pitiful not to be able to stay in the one place that always made me feel like me."

"You'll find your way back to you," she says, like it's a fact, then takes the last bite of her cookie.

"What if I can't?"

"You will." She clears her throat. "But the you that you're looking for may not be on the field." Then she starts the car, and I stare out the window at my team.

There are two other people at physical therapy, a woman with an ankle injury and a kid wearing a Boston University sweatshirt with his arm in a sling. They wave when I arrive.

My body's tired, but Waylan is so happy about the littlest things I can do—like taking two steps on the parallel bars and holding a fork with a giant foam piece around it. I'm glad I can do this stuff, but being excited about it feels ridiculous. I mean, Mo'ne Davis never would've nailed the 70 mph fastball and been the first girl to pitch a shutout in Little League World Series history by being okay with just doing the small stuff.

I want every stupid thing to stop being so hard. To stop hurting.

But it never does. So I'm just mad at my body. Which I didn't know was a thing you could be mad at.

29
Sideways

I check my email. No response yet from the remote-control-car company. My brain tangles. Why haven't they written back? It's rude.

I pace around my room. I hate waiting. I'm pretty terrible at it. Actually, I remember Mr. Jennings, my fourth-grade teacher, telling Mom and Dad during parent-teacher conferences that patience was something I needed to work on. Along with being less distracted by everything. Forgetting less. And finishing my homework more.

He always wanted me to be more like Geneva and her color-coded notebook. Or Wren, with their stack of library books. Or Liam, with his intricate graphs. Or anyone else, really.

I pick up my gerbil, Tony, and pet the soft brown fur down his back, then do the same with my other gerbil, Stark. I already know I can't let this go. I can't leave it alone. Because Dani's wrong. I do care about stuff. Maybe not the way she does. Maybe not the way most people do. Like, I don't care about homework or a clean room. Unless it's part of a promise. But I do care about doing the right thing. And it turns out, I'm a pretty good leader. Which means I need to do something. I can't let this go, even if Dani wants me to. Because it's not about me and her anymore. It's bigger than that. It's bigger than us.

But sometimes when I commit, I get lost down a rabbit hole that leads to another rabbit hole and another, and then I forget where I started. That's what happened this summer when Dani was away at baseball camp. I was going to create my own comic book and surprise her with it when she came home. I spent days and days looking up superheroes. There was Iron Man, Mystique, Captain America, Black Panther, Groot, Star Lord, Wolverine, Batman, Robin, Superman, Spider-Man, Loki, Doctor Strange. These were just the ones I started with. Then I did the deep dive into powers: flight, telekinesis, strength, healing, disguise, shape-shifting, powered armor suits, agility, genius, speed, web shooting. The problem was, one superhero led to another and another. Which led to powers and more powers, and analyzing which one was best. By the time Dani came home, I had a notebook full of lists of superheroes and powers, but no comic.

Just a lot of rabbit holes.

But there are other times when I commit to something and I find *the* way. And it's the way most people miss, because they're looking at things from only one direction. That's the part Mr. Jennings never got. He never understood that I was down the rabbit hole looking at the problem from lots of different directions: upside down, inside out, and sideways.

Sometimes upside down, inside out, and sideways is exactly where the answer is.

I actually think *this* may be my superpower.

Even if no one believes me.

I pace around my room. I have to do something, because I may never hear back from the remote-control-car company.

I pace some more.

Until I have an idea.

Then I text Rachel and head to her house.

"Hi," Rachel says when she opens the door, tucking her hair behind her ear so I can see her purple-stone earring.

"Hey. Turns out, you may have been right. I haven't heard back from RCarz. Maybe they don't care about some kid, but I have another idea."

She takes my hand and I try to walk like a normal person while every neuron in my brain's firing.

She leads me into the kitchen that smells like nothing. Not cookies or meatballs or onions or fish. It's like no one has ever cooked in here.

"What's your new idea?" she says as she grabs Oreos, a bag of chips, and her laptop. She takes an Oreo, opens it, and eats the creamy middle.

"We force them to listen." I stick my hand in the bag and grab a bunch of jalapeño chips.

"How?"

"We do a story or create a petition or something like that for Speak Out! We tell everyone what happened to Dani and that it was the company's fault, and that we wrote to them and they ignored us when we asked for their help." I take a breath. "You know, something bigger than one email from one kid. Something they can't ignore." I cross my fingers behind my back and hope she thinks this is a good plan.

"I like it," Rachel says, her green eyes getting big.

My relief comes out as an embarrassingly loud exhale. "Thanks."

Rachel leans over the table. "Let's email Ms. Suarez and tell her your idea."

"Yes!" I say.

"But if she agrees, and I totally think she will, she's going to ask if you've talked to Dani and gotten her permission.

Remember Ms. Suarez told us that last year she refused to run a story when a writer didn't get permission from the main source? She's a stickler for that kind of thing, so you probably want to do that first."

I nod, although I was hoping to do this without talking to Dani.

Rachel and I make a list of stuff we want to include in the piece if Ms. Suarez says yes. Then Rachel's mom walks in, carrying a tennis racket and wearing all white, followed by her dad, dressed in a navy suit with a skinny tie and holding a leather briefcase. I've seen them before around the neighborhood, but I've never really talked to them.

"Nice to meet you, Eric," Rachel's dad says, extending his hand, which fully wraps around mine. He's got curly hair, is super tall, and is wearing black loafers with a silver buckle.

"You too." I tuck in my T-shirt with the relish stain from today's delicious hot dog.

"Rachel tells me you guys are members of the social action club at school." He puts his briefcase on the kitchen chair next to me. "That's great. What are you working on?"

"Safety stuff mostly. We actually want to talk about the explosion at the campground this past summer." The word *explosion* sticks on my tongue as the images of that morning snake into my brain.

Rachel's dad nods, glances at Rachel's mom, and grabs some chips from our snack supply. "Really?"

"Yeah. Not sure if you heard about it. But it was bad and my friend Dani got hurt."

"Hmm. That's a real shame," he says.

"But we have to get permission from the teacher who runs the club," Rachel adds.

"This type of activism will look great on your private school application, honey," her mom says, waving the tennis racket in the air.

Rachel gives her mom a look I recognize. It's the kind I give my dad when I'm between embarrassed and annoyed.

"Oh. Are you changing schools?" I ask Rachel.

"Falcon Hill is a prestigious all-girl private school, and it's a feeder to Falcon High, which is a feeder to most Ivy League colleges," her dad says before she can answer.

"Wow, college," I say. "That's, like, a lot of years from now."

"It's never too early for my girl to start thinking about these things," Mr. Kent says. "And this incident on the Cape will make a great story."

"Well, it's not a story. I mean, it's real. It happened. To me and my friend."

Or once friend.

"Of course," he says in a brushing-me-off kind of way. "But if your school doesn't want it, there are essay contests you can enter. You can write in to the newspaper." Then he turns to Rachel. "Or, even better, you could write about it in your application essay," he says, smiling at Rachel.

I tap my sneaker on the wood floor and fidget in my chair. "Um, what happened at the Cape is personal," I say. "Like, it *actually* happened. It's not some random thing Rachel can just use on her application."

Rachel says nothing.

30

Loser

The school cafeteria is crowded. My body feels hot in my wheelchair, and the cast on my leg is making my skin itch. I try shifting my mind away from the itchiness toward lunch, but it's not working.

Meadow looks my way and holds out a pink lemonade. I give her a thumbs-up and motion toward the chocolate chip cookies.

While I'm waiting at the long table, Eric plops down next to me. "Can we talk?"

"Sounds like you're breaking up with me." I smile and look at my newly polished nails. They're pink, except my ring fingers. Those are blue. Meadow did them for me.

Eric glances around. "Can we go somewhere else?"

I shake my head and point to Meadow, who's getting my lunch.

He sighs and lowers his voice. "I have this idea, and since it involves you, I kind of need to tell you."

I stare at him. "Thought you were done saving me?" My words are sharp.

Eric puts his hand on his bouncing knee. "Look, you don't get to be a jerk just because you got hurt."

"Ouch!"

"And if I'm being honest," his knee speeds up, "I don't want to be here any more than you want me to be. So just hear me out, then I'll take off." He opens his chocolate milk and takes a swig.

"I'm listening."

Meadow holds up a burger from the lunch line, and I nod.

"I want to do a story or something for Speak Out! about what happened that morning at the Cape."

"Why?" I snap.

"So what happened to you doesn't happen to anyone else. Like the guy with the lawn mower. Remember him, from that show we saw?"

My frustration sparks. "Can't you just forget about it? Like everything else you've ever not done?"

He shakes his head. "Look, we can help a lot of people. Just think about it."

"Fine," I say wanting to end this conversation. Then I see Rachel wave to Eric, and his face turns red.

"What's going on with you guys?" I ask, kind of surprised I don't know.

"We've been hanging out." He smiles at Rachel, then tosses his empty chocolate milk carton toward the garbage can. It lands on the floor.

McKinnon and the team walk past my table. I wave with my left hand, my right on my lap like it's a choice. They nod and keep walking.

My insides hollow.

Meadow comes over with my lunch. She puts down the tray. "Thanks," I say.

She smiles at me, then turns to Eric and in a super loud voice says, "This loser bothering you?" as she settles into the now-full table.

Kids laugh.

Somewhere in the background I hear Leo loudly chanting, "Loser! Loser! Loser!"

Eric waits for me to defend him.

But I don't.

I see the hurt seep across his face. I bite the inside of my cheek and twirl his lucky coin in my pocket.

I should do something. Say something. But my words stick.

I close my eyes and imagine my old life.

And when I open them, Eric's gone.

31

True Enough

Two days have gone by.

No apology. No "Wow, I've been the world's biggest jerk!"

Nothing.

How could Dani sit there and let Meadow call me a loser in front of everyone?

I open and close my shutters three times. Before all this, that was my and Dani's emergency signal to meet at our windows. I do it one more time. But again . . . nothing.

I leave the window, give Tony and Stark some yogurt treats, and check my school email. Turns out after all that, Ms. Suarez isn't a fan of sharing Dani's story through Speak

Out! Something about school policy barring the school from lobbying against a privately held company.

No. No. No. I go downstairs. The thump of the laundry machine fills the kitchen. Zoe looks up. She's wearing her newest princess crown and coloring. I eat an entire row of Oreos, hoping to find answers in the creamy filling. But all I find is that eating that many Oreos gives me a stomachache.

Aunt Josie walks in and eyes the missing row of cookies. "Something you want to talk about?"

I shrug. "I'm trying to do something good, but I keep making things worse, and now I don't know what to do."

"If this is important to you, Eric, keep going. You'll find a way in." She hugs me tight. "I promise."

"How do you know?"

"Because we're a lot alike, you and me, and that scattered part of us that can sometimes be a total pain is also the part that never gives up on the things or people who matter most."

Maybe she's right. Maybe I can do this.

"Thanks, Aunt Josie." I go back to my room and text Rachel what Ms. Suarez said. She's as mad as I am. We decide to figure out our next move at her house.

Before I leave, I sprinkle some powder on my palms.

When I see Rachel, she's wearing this aqua shirt.

"Hi," I say, thankful she can't see my brain and all its feelings.

We go into the family room and sit on a velvety tan

couch. The kind you'd see in a fancy hotel and be too afraid to sit on. The dogs follow.

"Look, about the other day and the whole application thing. You get it, right?" I say, petting Milo.

"Yeah. It's just my dad. He gets a little overeager about this stuff."

"I mean, some of the things I told you about that morning were, um, private. You know? Like, I wouldn't want them ending up in an essay."

Rachel nods. "I totally get it."

A rush of relief comes over me.

She inches a little closer, and I don't want to move.

Ever.

But then Rachel starts talking about next steps and gets up to grab her laptop.

We need more information to find a way to get the manufacturer to stop selling the defective remote-control cars.

We start by searching the company online again. A bunch of YouTube videos pop up. One is of a similar car that starts a small fire with a bunch of teenagers, but no one gets hurt. The other is like that, but with two old dudes. However, I can't tell in either video if the car is the same as the remote-control camper we had.

We do a broader search, and something called the Consumer Product Safety Commission, or CPSC, comes up. Says it's a government agency that's about keeping people safe. There are links on its homepage: "Report Unsafe Products."

"Search Unsafe Products." I click on "Report" first and put in all the information I know about the car and the explosion and hit Submit.

Then I click on Search.

Four results.

"I still can't tell if any of these are the same model or, really, what this stuff means," I say.

"Look," Rachel says, pointing to something called a Freedom of Information Act Request. "You can put in the information you have, ask about other injuries, and it'll send you what they know. Maybe if there are enough injuries, we can contact the news station or *The Clippings,* and then the car company will have to listen."

Yes!

I find an email address I can send the request to instead of filing the form. There's a fee if I file, but the email is free. I put in the information and hit Send. Then I scroll down the page and in small print see that if we're lucky, we'll get a response in weeks, but most likely months or longer.

I stare at the words as frustration steals my hope.

32
Something I Was

For the past few days, Meadow's been trying to convince me that I need to celebrate. "It's your birthday. It's been, like, a month since the accident. You can't hide in your house forever. You have to do something other than just school."

Yesterday I finally gave in.

"The party is going to be so much fun," she says, while I lie on my back lifting and lowering my leg. Waylan told me when I can walk all the way across the parallel bars, I can ditch the walker and graduate to forearm crutches. So I've been doing my PT a lot in hopes of speeding up my graduation date.

"Your fans will be here soon." Meadow laughs.

"What fans?" I sit up.

She hands me her phone. "See?" She points to the thousand-plus people following us on TikTok.

"Wow," I say. "When did that happen? Last time I checked, there were maybe thirty followers. I was pretty sure half were related to you and the other half had crushes on you."

"After our last post, they started following. You totally nailed it."

I fake-smile, hiding the flash of nausea shooting through my body. That post was a Say It about Eric, or me and Eric, and the whole *loser* comment. Meadow brought it up while we were videotaping. "Dani, tell everyone what really happened," she said.

I remember the long silence that surrounded her words. I couldn't speak. It was as if haze had snatched my brain. Meadow looked at me with wide eyes, like *Aren't you going to say something?* But I didn't. So she filled the uncomfortable silence with a lot of words.

Some true.

Most not.

All hurtful.

But *I* never said Eric was a loser. I wouldn't do that. He's my friend. Or was. Or whatever. I just wouldn't. But I never said he wasn't either. And that's the part that makes me feel like I'm turning into someone Gigi would be disappointed in.

When she was alive, I could almost handle her being mad at me. But the whole "I'm disappointed in you, Dani" always felt way worse. Like the thing she was upset about wasn't something I did but something I was.

I should have spoken up when Meadow called Eric a loser that day in the cafeteria. But I was so frustrated with him treating me like some stupid cause that I let the words float in the air for everyone to hear. Then when she said, "Right, Dani?" I just said, "Yeah. Let's move on." And we did. Leaving the loser thing to live forever.

She holds up a pink shirt with sparkles that is definitely not something she found in my closet.

"I got this for you to wear to the party. It slides over your head, so you don't have to worry about buttoning it."

I stare at Meadow and wonder how she can be so thoughtful with me and so obnoxious to Eric. I've always assumed people were either good or bad. I didn't think there were in-betweeners. But Meadow's definitely an in-betweener.

She hands me the shirt, and I use my good arm to glide it over the bad one. I've gotten better at this. Now I can even move my right arm a bit, and there's less numbness in my hand, but my shoulder still hurts when I put anything over my head.

"You look totally cute." She takes her rhinestone-decorated hand mirror out of her bag and shows me.

I stare at the person looking back at me. The person I used to know. The one who had a best friend named Eric and hated pink.

I realize that I barely know this person, but I smile anyway. "Thanks."

Meadow hands me the walker, and we move into the family room onto the ugly couch.

Someone knocks. Casey runs to the door, and Meadow answers it. Her little sister and her mom walk in. "They wanted to wish you a happy birthday before everyone gets here."

"Happy Birthday, Dani." Millie hands me a homemade card covered with smiley face stickers. "Look what I can do," she says as she wiggles the fingers on her injured hand.

"Great job," I say, petting Casey, who's sniffing the floor for crumbs.

She smiles, then plops down next to me. "I think you're really brave."

"Well, I think you're brave, too," I tell her.

"You know what else?" she says, taking a gingerbread cookie from the plate Mom left out earlier.

"What?"

"I'm not even mad at Meadow anymore," she says. "And I was pretty mad."

"Oh. Well, that's good." I don't really get why she'd be mad at Meadow. I mean, Meadow was with her all the time at the hospital.

Meadow walks over. "Don't you guys need to go?"

Millie looks at me and then at her big sister. She finishes her cookie and gives me a hug good-bye.

I pet Casey, who's snuggled next to me, and ask Meadow, "What did your sister mean?"

"Nothing," she says, rolling her eyes. "Let's just celebrate your birthday."

The doorbell rings.

Casey barks as Meadow's mom and little sister leave and Meadow's friends Taylor, Brie, Kya, and Jojo come in.

"Happy birthday," my new sort-of friends say at once. Kya and Jojo dig into the plate of cookies. Brie immediately starts talking about this kid in English she has a crush on.

Brie finds the kid's pic and sweeps her phone across the room.

"Yep, definitely cute," Meadow says.

"Does anyone know the score of the Red Sox game?" I ask, scanning the room for my phone or another Sox fan.

I find neither.

The doorbell rings again. McKinnon and four others from my baseball team stroll in, and my heart drops.

"Surprise!" Meadow says, hooking her arm through the second baseman's. "Isn't this great?"

Then, in unison, my teammates say, "Happy birthday!"

"Thanks," I say, trying to hide how not-great this is.

I look at my teammates standing in my house.

I'm not ready.

Not ready.

Not ready.

Another knock at the door. I pray it's not more kids from the team. Meadow gets up.

Eric walks in.

I'm shocked he's here after everything, and the second I see him, my heart fills with things I should have said.

Casey runs over and jumps on him. Eric's wearing the gray, white, and red flannel we got together last fall. I have the same one in blue, white, and yellow. When we bought them, I said we were twins.

"I, um, didn't know you were having people over," he says, walking toward me. I can see the hurt behind his eyes.

Meadow steps in his path. "It's just something I put together for Dani's birthday," she says, like she's the friend who knows I sleep with my closet light on, that I don't like different foods on my plate to touch, and that I hate the smell of cantaloupe.

Don't hate me.

He ignores Meadow and comes over to me.

I'm sorry I let her call you a loser.

"I would have invited you but—"

"Don't," he snaps before the rest of my words trickle out. "Things are different now."

My heart aches. In this moment I know he's right. Things

are different. I'm different. We're different. And as much as I don't want Eric to feel bad, I'm not sure I can go back.

"I just stopped by to drop this off." He hands me a lumpy brown paper bag. "I thought you should have it."

As he turns around to leave, Meadow yells to the back of his shirt, "My cousin Leo says hi."

Eric hesitates for a moment but doesn't turn around.

A switch inside me flicks on.

But it's too late.

Eric's already walking out the door.

"Open it," Meadow says, sliding next to me.

"Later," I tell her, shaking my head.

"Aw, come on. Let's see what the loser got you," she says, and the people on the couch laugh.

I close my eyes. "You gotta stop, Meadow."

I know my words are too late, but at least I finally said them.

"Whatever," she says.

I open the paper bag with my left hand, and sitting in my lap is my baseball glove. I smile and hug Betty. The leather smells like mornings at the park with the giant red tub of baseballs.

It reminds me of me.

And a friend who knows my heart.

33

Forever Jerk

It's been a week since I walked in on the birthday party I wasn't invited to. Honestly, I thought Dani's jerkiness was temporary. I thought it was because her body hurt, not because she actually was a forever jerk. But now I think it's permanent.

Dani invited a bunch of kids she barely knows, never did anything about all that stuff Meadow said about me, and is now best friends with my bully's cousin. It's like she doesn't care. Like she never cared.

I've tried to make excuses for her, ignore the truth, but I finally know that I don't want to fix things with Dani anymore.

I don't like this version of my once best-friend.

The one I missed all summer.

The one I saved.

It's time to move on. No big confrontation in the cafeteria. No yelling phone call or angry texts.

She's changed.

I've changed.

We've changed.

Plus, Rachel's coming over and I want to focus on not messing that up.

>   Deodorant ✔
>   Powder ✔
>   Chapstick ✔
>   Body spray. On it.

When the doorbell rings, Zoe runs and opens the door. "Hi," she says, her voice bouncy. "Do you like princesses?"

"Sure," Rachel says, walking into my house for the first time.

"Who's your favorite?" Zoe straightens her crown. "Mine's Princess Jasmine."

"I like Princess Jasmine, too, but my favorite is Mulan."

"What about princes?"

I step between Zoe and Rachel. "Let's give Rachel some time to think about it. Okay, Peanut?"

Zoe stares at me. "You smell funny," she says, rubbing her nose.

My face burns with embarrassment. Trying to ignore my little sister, I turn to Rachel. "Hi."

"Hello," she says, following me to the tree fort in the backyard. Dani and I used to hang out here, but not since before baseball camp.

I open a box of donuts. Rachel takes a bite of a powdered one.

I pause, find my courage, lean over, and gently wipe the powder from her cheek. Then I hold her hand.

God, please let this not be weird.

Rachel smiles.

Not weird. Thank you.

We sit and talk like this for a while. Then we share her purple pen and finish the latest *Clippings* crossword puzzle together.

We dive into the comics I have. Some online and some of Dad's old-school paper ones.

Rachel picks up Dani's favorite Mystique comic. I watch as she reads it. She takes the last bite of her donut and says, "Not sure I really like Mystique."

I blink. "Why? She's cool." For some weird reason I feel like I need to defend Mystique.

"Well, she's a shape-shifter, right?"

I nod. "Yeah. That's what makes her so amazing. She can be anyone." Dani always said that about her.

"I guess," she says. "But it also makes her untrustworthy."

I lean forward. "How?"

She puts the comic back onto the stack. "If she can turn into anyone, then she's true to no one."

I never thought of it that way.

"I mean, who is she, really?"

My glazed donut sticks in my throat. Because I realize I can't answer that anymore.

34
Not My Fault

Casey lies next to me on Gigi's bedspread. We like it in here. I can still kind of smell her hairspray. It's the same and different all at once.

Feels like so much is different. Eric's mad and ignoring me. I spied him staring at me at school the other day when Meadow was helping me get to class. Part of me felt bad. He looked my way, caught my eye, then turned around and said nothing. I don't totally blame him.

The loser thing is still out there. I did apologize.

But only in my head.

Not sure that counts.

But the party wasn't my fault. I didn't have a birth-day thing and not invite him. Meadow did. That's on her. And the related-to-Leo thing, I mean, that's not my fault either.

If I'm being in-my-heart honest, though, there's a lot on me, too. The truth is, I miss him. I just don't know what to do about it. I don't know how to make things right. And for now Waylan says I need to focus all my energy on getting my body stronger.

What's left over has to deal with the giant scary thoughts swirling in my brain. The ones I keep tucked away. Like how any of this really ends. What if I do all the stuff Waylan says and I still can't play baseball? What if I never get all the feeling back in my hand? What if all the grown-ups are wrong and time doesn't magically fix everything?

All of it terrifies all of me.

"You ready?"

It's Mom, standing just outside the door of Gigi's room. She never comes in here.

"Yep," I say, stuffing my big, messy, confusing feelings away.

Mom drives me to physical therapy. The ride is quiet. I stare out the window and wonder about epic baseball play-ers like Lizzie Murphy and Mo'ne Davis and if they ever felt the kind of scared that floods you with doubt.

When we get to PT, I grab my walker. I mostly just need the wheelchair at school now. Waylan doesn't want kids bumping into me. Yesterday I had an X-ray and other imaging, and Dr. Jeffries said the bone in my leg is healing well. Even my hand and arm are getting stronger. Less tingling, more listening to my brain.

Mom heads to the coffee shop to work while I go into the room that smells like feet.

Waylan's setting up the PT table. "Hello, my friend. I'm feeling optimistic about today," he says, smiling.

His happiness and hope are almost contagious, but the throbbing that slides down my leg is getting in the way.

Waylan helps me onto the table and counts my leg raises, telling me what a great job I'm doing. "If you couldn't be a physical therapist, what would you do?" I ask, trying to ignore how hard it still feels to raise and lower my right leg.

I've been thinking about this a lot. Did Waylan always want to be a physical therapist? Did Coach Levi always want to be a baseball coach? And Dr. Jeffries and the guy at the grocery store. Is what they're doing now what they've always wanted to be? Or was there some other version?

Waylan laughs. "Being a physical therapist was not my first love."

I'm surprised, because I can't imagine him doing anything else. This job fits him.

"I ran hurdles in college and had big dreams. Then I tore my ACL playing basketball with some friends. That was it. There was no way I could still run hurdles competitively. It just hurt too much. I had a choice: pain or pivot. I chose pivot. Do what I could to help others."

"Like me."

He nods. "Chin up, my young friend," he says. "It all turns out okay in the end, I promise. Look at me, I'm happy."

I nod and swallow. "Do you ever get mad that you can't run hurdles anymore?"

"Sure. Tearing my ACL took something away from me. Something that was important to me. But now I look around and see where I ended up. If I'd run hurdles, I wouldn't be here. I wouldn't have met you. I wouldn't have found this part of me."

We move to the parallel bars, and I clench my teeth.

"You've got this, Dani. Remember, you get to choose. Life is not happening to you."

"Sometimes it feels that way, though. Like these bad things happened and I was powerless."

Waylan leans in. "But you're not. You may not get to choose what sport you play or when you get to play it, but you get to choose who you are. And in the end, that's what matters most."

I ready myself on the parallel bars and walk. It's hard, but I'm doing it. My hand grips in a way it hasn't, and my leg feels stronger. I don't make it all the way across, but I go farther than I've gone before.

And that's a win.

I look at my empty bangle bracelet and wonder what part of me I'll find.

35

Radio Silence

Feels weird going so long without talking to Dani. Even when she was at baseball camp, we texted. The last text I sent said, *One More Day!* She replied with a happy face, a thumbs-up, and a goat.

Now there's nothing. No texts. No emojis. Just silence.

After school I lace up my sneakers and go for a run. The blue skies follow me down the path. My breath quickens. I don't stop. My frustration pounds my chest as my sneakers slap the pavement.

Dani's wrong about me.

I don't forget everything.

I'm not a loser.

That's *my* truth.

I stop for a minute and look up. *Thanks, God. I know you're with me on this one.*

I cut across the park and through the winding streets of the neighborhood. The sweat burns my eyes. My legs shake. I rest on the curb.

My head's in my hands when I feel a dog's cold nose nudge me. It's Oscar, Jade Zhang's gray-and-white mutt. When Oscar was a puppy, he'd escape to our house every morning. Mom said it was because he loved us. I think it was because Zoe left half her breakfast for him in our backyard.

"Hey, Eric," Jade says.

"Hi."

"I heard Dani's improving," she says. "That's great." Her wire-rim glasses reflect the sun, and she moves over to the shady part of the street.

"Yep."

Jade sits on the curb next to me. "That's the face your dad makes when our softball team is down by five in the bottom of the ninth with two outs. What's going on?"

"Nothing," I say.

She raises her right eyebrow.

"Well, sort of everything."

She gives Oscar a treat from her pocket and listens.

"I tried doing this thing to help Dani, but it didn't work. Then I tried doing this other thing to, you know, do something good, but that also didn't work. Now it's all messed up."

It doesn't take long for me to unload my horribly unsuccessful plan. I think getting people to talk like this is some kind of investigative-reporter thing. She nods as I tell her about the email the remote-control-car company ignored, Ms. Suarez's refusal to do the story, and the request through the Freedom of Information Act that will take forever. The words pour out like a kicked-over bucket of water.

She listens, pets Oscar, and says nothing.

I fidget, crack my knuckles, and try to find my hangnail.

I said too much. I'm an idiot.

"When I was a kid, I camped in East Mapleville with my parents, just like you guys do," Jade says. "It's a special place."

"That's cool," I say. "So you get it."

She nods, and as I sit there, an idea zips into my brain. Then I draw in a giant breath to find my courage. "Um, maybe you could help," I say. "I mean, you make that podcast my dad listens to, right?"

"I do."

"Maybe you could do, like, a story or something about what happened."

"Hmm. Interesting idea."

"Would you?" I ask as possibility replaces the stench of failure attached to me.

She nods. "We do that a lot. Tell stories that impact the people who live in our community." She stands. "I'll run it by my producer and talk to Dani and her family. But if I get permission from everyone, then we've got a story."

"We?" I ask.

"Yeah, why don't you help me out?"

I wipe my sticky forehead. "Are you serious?"

"As long as your parents say it's okay, who better to help tell this story than Dani's best friend?"

Definitely not Dani's best friend anymore.

She gives Oscar another treat. "But, full disclosure, there's a stack of papers on my desk, and I'm behind on everything." She laughs. "While you're too young to officially intern, you're free to come by the office and pitch in, and I'll show you around. How does that sound?"

"Great!"

"All right. I'll reach out to my producer. You talk to your parents and let the Meyers know I'll be in touch to see if they're interested."

My mind spins with the thought of talking to Dani about another plan or, really, anything.

But as I head toward the path by Cutter Park to finish my run, hope slides in, and I break into my victory dance.

Then I take a left instead of a right and run to Rachel's. I knock and am thinking maybe I should have showered first when the front door opens.

Rachel smiles and I forget about the sweat rolling down my back.

The good news rushes out of me. "You're not going to believe this, but Jade Zhang agreed, or almost agreed, to tell Dani's story on her podcast. Or at least she offered to if her producer person and Dani and her mom say it's okay."

"That's amazing, Eric."

"What's amazing?" her dad asks, walking into the hallway.

"Eric got Jade Zhang to talk on her podcast about what happened to Dani this summer," Rachel says.

Mr. Kent rests his arm on his daughter's shoulder. "Honey, this is fantastic news. I'm happy Dani's story will be out there." He snaps his fingers. "Rachel, you should have Eric read your essay."

"What essay?" I ask Rachel.

She looks away.

"You said you weren't going to write about it," I say, a bad feeling crawling across my chest. I thought she got it. I thought she understood that this wasn't just some story to use to get into private school.

"Rachel, you really should have Eric read it."

Rachel's face turns crimson.

Then, standing there in the hallway with Rachel begging him not to, Mr. Kent pulls up Rachel's private school application essay on his phone and hands it to me to read. "I mean, she writes so beautifully, and there's so much detail. You would have thought she was there that day."

He's right, it is well written and filled with all the details I shared with her in private.

It is like she was there. At the explosion. That morning.

But she wasn't.

I was.

36
My Old Life

Meadow comes back to my house after school. She kicks off her sneakers with the pink stars and sits next to me on the ugly couch. I'm doing my hand exercises with the harder, stronger red band.

"What did Millie mean when she said that stuff at my birthday party?" I ask her for like the fifth time. She's been avoiding answering me. She keeps saying that she's too tired to talk about it, not in the mood, I'm making a big deal about nothing, too much homework.

"Can't we just eat your mom's blueberry muffins and drop it?" She puts one on her napkin.

"We can eat the muffins, but . . ." I sigh. Maybe it isn't anything, but the more she avoids it, the more I want to know. "All I want to know is what your sister meant when she said that she wasn't mad at you anymore."

For a long minute all I hear is the hum of the dishwasher as I open and close my fingers. Then Meadow says, "It was nothing, really."

"So stop dodging the question and just answer it," I say, removing the band.

"Siblings fight about dumb stuff. You're lucky you're an only child."

I grab the putty and start the next exercise.

"She was mad at me and now she's not. It happens with sisters."

"But *why* was she mad? You were totally there for her." This is so confusing to me. I 100 percent don't get siblings.

"She's little. Not everything she does makes sense."

I squeeze the putty as Casey tries to nose it out of my hand. "But that's not fair. If she was mad at anyone, I'd think it'd be your brother. It was his fault."

Meadow doesn't respond.

I put the putty down. It takes me a few slow minutes to grab my phone and turn on the camera. "Time for another edition of Say It or Do It with Dani and Meadow."

"What are you doing?" Meadow asks in a nervous whisper.

"Trust me," I say.

Her chestnut-brown eyes widen as I hit Record.

"Okay, friends, here we go. No worries, Meadow, I promise I won't cut your hair. But I have a Say It for you, so you can sort something out for all of us." I take in a deep, nervous breath. "What was your brother doing when he accidentally slammed your sister's hand in the car door? Texting? Eating chips? Talking to his girlfriend?"

"Don't, Dani," she says.

"Come on, Meadow. It's time to set the record straight." I wink and whisper to her, "You can thank me later." Casey yawns and stretches by my feet.

"I can't do this," Meadow says.

"Sure, you can. Just be honest. It's okay." I nod to my friend.

"Dani, turn it off. Turn it off!" she yells.

I stare at her.

"Okay, more later," I say as I stop recording.

"Why would you do that?" Meadow's voice is accusing.

"I was trying to help."

Meadow doesn't move or say anything. Then, "He didn't do it."

"What do you mean?"

Her eyes brim with tears. "I did it, Dani. It was me."

I stare at her. "But you said *he* slammed Millie's hand in the car door. That *he* should feel bad for what he did." My mind races. I knew her sister said she wasn't mad at

Meadow anymore, but I never thought *this* was what she was talking about. I never thought Meadow would lie to me like that.

"The accident was my fault. Not my brother's." She pauses and stands. "Now you know. And it doesn't matter if Millie forgives me, because *I* don't forgive me." Tears roll down her cheeks. I've never seen Meadow cry. Her face looks different.

"I get that you're upset, and I'm sorry for that. But you lied to me and then said all that horrible stuff about Eric, the explosion, and my injuries being his fault. Him being a terrible person. Him lying. Why did you do that?"

She's quiet.

The pieces come together in a bad way. I believed her. I listened to her. I followed her like a shadow down an alley. I was so desperate to be friends with one of the most popular girls in school, I'd believe anything. Do anything. Say anything.

My heart sinks.

"I'm sorry, Dani." She puts the half-eaten muffin and napkin on the table and walks out the door.

I hug Betty, my baseball glove.

My brain spins. Everything's so confusing. Meadow's not the person I thought she was. She's the person Eric knew she was.

My eyes sting.

I miss my old life.

Tears hit my lap.

I miss me.

I spin my lucky coin in my hands and realize I miss Eric, too. His skinny arms. His scary stories. Even his hands-down wrong opinion that Iron Man is the best superhero to ever live.

"Want some?" It's Mom with two glasses of iced tea.

I nod.

She sits next to me. "You okay?"

I shake my head and lean into her. She smells like vanilla.

"How much did you hear?" I ask.

"All of it," she says. "I was baking, not eavesdropping, but the house is small and voices carry through the archway."

I know that's true, because I used to hear her and Gigi talking in the kitchen long after I was supposed to be sleeping.

"I'm sorry this is all so hard," she says, staring out the window.

I look at my mom and remember the last time we just sat and talked. Gigi was sick. Like, puking and rambling kind of sick. Mom sat me down with a plate of gingerbread cookies and told me that Gigi wasn't getting better. That's the first time I realized that not everything can be fixed with cookies and love.

"Why would Meadow lie?"

"I don't know. People do things for all sorts of reasons."

"Like they're jerks."

"Maybe. Maybe not. Maybe there's something else going on that you don't know about. Something she's working through." She looks at me. "No one gets it right all the time. We all make mistakes."

I think about Eric and me and the things I did and didn't do.

"It's what we do after those mistakes that counts." Mom leans in. "I love you, Dani."

I nod, because I'm afraid words will stop her from talking.

"I know I don't say it enough, but I do. The truth is, ever since Gigi got sick, I've had a hard time with things I can't control. Like losing her, your accident, and all the worries and fears attached to those circumstances." She exhales. "But I'm working on it. I promise."

"I kind of thought you just hated baseball."

She smiles and tucks my hair behind my ear. "I don't hate baseball. I'm sorry you thought that. And I'm very proud of you."

I rest my head on my mom's shoulder.

We sit together quietly for a while. She points to my baseball glove. "Something else Eric saved?"

Her words pull at me, and I nod. Then my phone buzzes. Mom kisses my forehead and leaves the room.

"Hello," I say.

"Hey." Eric's voice cracks.

It sounds like him, but not really. It's like his goofiness has been wiped clean, and now there's no sign of the Eric I know. The one who saved me. The one I hurt.

"I wanted to tell you about this offer thing from Jade Zhang."

"The podcast person from the temple softball team?" I ask.

"Yeah. She has that weekly show and wants to talk to you and your mom about maybe doing a feature on what happened to you this summer."

"Oh."

"You guys need to call her and let her know if you're interested. It's up to you."

"Okay," I say, catching a glimpse of my reflection in the mirror.

What do I want?

Eric gives me Jade Zhang's telephone number and hangs up.

I wonder why he's still trying to help.

After all the stuff I didn't say.

37
More to the Story

I thought Rachel understood this wasn't just some story to use to get into private school.

Last night she texted: *Sorry don't be mad*

I didn't text back.

I don't have history or a club meeting and somehow manage to get through today without bumping into her at school.

I bolt when the final bell rings. It's my first day at the radio station helping Jade. She said she spoke to Alice and they're all in.

And since I'm now a believer that donuts are the key to

everything, I make a quick stop at Anna's Bakery to grab a dozen.

Before going into Jade's office, I eat a glazed donut and reread what I wrote for her. She said she'd get the facts about the company involved and all the government regulations, but she wants to know my side of things, what I experienced. So last night, after reading *Our Friend Hedgehog: The Story of Us* (three times) and *I'm Sorry* (four times) to Zoe, I tried to write while Tony and Stark spun on their wheel.

But I just couldn't get the words out. Instead I watched *Iron Man* while the story of the accident swam in my head. This morning I tried again. I thought about texting Rachel, but even I knew that was a bad idea. I wrote and deleted and wrote and deleted and wrote some more. I sat in my chair, my leg jitter bobbing, and read aloud to the gerbils.

Our annual camping trip started great. I was at the Cape with my best friend, Dani, and my dad. The first day I woke up early, wrapped myself in my sleeping bag, and left the camper.

Within minutes I heard a loud boom. Fire, smoke, and bits of glass, paper, and cloth were everywhere. My dad was out fishing, but Dani was trapped inside the camper. I ran in and found her stuck under a bunch of cabinets, surrounded by thick smoke. I dragged her out. I was really scared.

By seven o'clock in the morning, I knew this was the worst day of my life.

Dani was hurt. Her right leg and arm were injured. Dani is right-handed. Dani's a baseball pitcher.

Recently we found out that the explosion was caused by some defect in my remote-control car. The car was made by RCarz. I emailed the company to tell them what happened, hoping they'd help make sure this never happens to anyone else.

But the company never got back to me.

RCarz shouldn't be allowed to ignore kids who get hurt using their stuff. A company shouldn't be allowed to hide from the truth.

I put my phone back into my pocket and walk through the revolving door of Jade's office building. I take the elevator to the sixth floor. The elevator doors open, and I immediately love this place. It feels alive. Jade is waiting for me. As we walk down the hall we pass a guy wearing a Celtics hat in a control room surrounded by a giant board with sliders and buttons. There are recording booths with microphones and lots of desks for reporters. Jade introduces me around. The donuts turn out to be a good idea.

When we get to Jade's desk, it's a mess, like mine. Which, oddly, makes me happy. But her piles make her mess look more purposeful.

She asks me questions about that morning and records my answers. I use what I wrote to help me say what's spinning in my brain. Then she holds up an envelope with CPSC on it. I recognize the initials, and my heart speeds up.

"It's the results from your Freedom of Information Act request," she tells me. "I had a guy I know who works there fast-track your request and send the results here." She takes out the letter and hands it to me. I try to read it but it doesn't make any sense, because most of the words are crossed out with big black lines.

"They're trying to protect the company," Jade explains when I look up, confused.

"I thought the whole point of the CPSC was to protect the people who use the company's stuff?"

"It is, but sometimes there are loopholes." Jade takes a sip from the water bottle on her desk.

"What happens now?"

Please don't say, "Nothing more we can do."

She stands up and grabs her jacket and a tote bag. "I did some digging, learned some new information, and have more to share."

"What did you find out?"

She heads out the door. I follow but need to walk fast to keep up.

"I spoke to Alice, and we're heading there now," she tells me as we enter the elevator.

"Why?" My body freezes. Because other than my giving her the information to call Jade, Dani and I aren't really talking.

Jade's face is serious. "There's a lot more to this story, Eric."

38

The Biggest One

I'm sitting in the family room with Mom and Casey when Eric walks in with Jade Zhang.

Last night Mom and I agreed to meet with Ms. Zhang and do this story. Then Mom nervous-baked peanut butter cookies, sugar cookies, and pumpkin muffins (in case Ms. Zhang's not a cookie person).

Casey runs over to Eric, who gives her some love, and then Eric looks at me. I didn't realize he'd be here, too. His curls fall in his face, and an uncomfortable silence edges between us. It feels strange. He's been my best friend since forever. He gave me his lucky coin. He knows my heart. He knows my secrets.

Except the biggest one, which nobody knows. That ever since the accident, there's a giant piece of me that's scared all the time.

I should tell him.

But maybe I should apologize first.

Ms. Zhang interrupts my brain spiral. "Thanks for agreeing to meet."

I run my hand through my short hair.

She sits across from us, and Mom offers her something to eat. Turns out she *is* a cookie person. She takes a peanut butter one. "What happened to you should never have happened, and maybe together we can make sure it never happens again."

I glance at Eric, who's staring at his sneakers. This is exactly what he's been saying all along.

"Ms. Zhang, we appreciate your coming here today," Mom says, sitting back down.

"You can call me Jade. I'm neither that old nor that formal yet."

Mom gives her a polite smile.

"There's information I need to share with you." Jade clears her throat. "I've been researching RCarz—the remote-control-car company—and I've learned that Dani's accident wasn't the first."

My eyes snap into laser mode.

That can't be true.

"What do you mean?" Mom asks, clasping her hands tightly.

"I did some digging and found that over the years RCarz has received numerous complaints, which range from smoke to sparks to small fires." She pauses and my chest squeezes.

"If that toy car started all those fires, why was it still for sale?" Mom asks, her voice as sharp as glass.

"Not sure. I don't have all the facts yet," Jade says, tightening the scarf tied around her neck.

My world is spinning. None of this makes sense. "I thought the explosion was an accident," I say. The room feels hot. Too hot. "Now you're telling me this has happened before. The company *knew* their remote-control cars could start fires and did nothing about it?"

Silence ricochets off the walls.

No one moves.

My stomach drops.

"This is outrageous," Mom says.

"Agreed," says Jade, nodding.

Casey comes over and lays her head in my lap like she's trying to protect me from stuff that's unfair.

"What happens now?" I ask Jade.

"We unbury the truth. The company can't hide forever."

My brain floods with angry thoughts, and I wonder what's worse: thinking that the explosion that derailed my life was a horrible accident or knowing that someone may have had the power to prevent it and didn't.

39

Sticky Floor

Back at home I call Big Al's Consignment Shop, where Dad bought our remote-control camper. I'm curious to know whether they've heard anything about these cars catching fire.

Big Al himself answers the phone. I ask him about the dangerous remote-control car and whether he knew about prior accidents or fires. His voice is deep. "Never heard about any trouble they were having with those cars. I wouldn't have sold them if I knew."

I keep going. I find another place that sells a different brand of remote-control cars and call them. A lady named Regina, who won't give me her last name, says she heard about the fires with the RCarz and tells me that she doesn't understand why they were even using those batteries. "I'm probably not supposed to be saying this, but there were newer lithium-ion batteries on the market at that time that were much safer. Pretty sure those batteries wouldn't have blown everything up."

I write down what she says as fast as I can so I can tell Jade what I found out.

I thank Regina and hang up, wondering why RCarz didn't just use the better batteries.

Jade forwarded some emails to me, and I start to read them. The first is from a guy who works in the engineering department of RCarz. No idea how Jade got this, but I assume it's another investigative reporter thing. It's dated well before the fire that hurt Dani.

> To: Charles Baniker
> Re: safety issue with remote-control cars
>
> Charles,
>
> After testing and research, I recommend that we switch to the newly designed lithium-ion batteries for our remote-control cars. They're safer. They won't overheat. Much lower fire potential.
>
> Reggie Masters
> Chief Engineer
> RCarz
> 100 Pioneer Way
> Seattle, WA

The next email is the reply from the head of the company.

To: Reggie Masters
Re: safety issue with remote-control cars

Reggie,

   Hold off on any safety changes at this time as the
newly designed batteries are too expensive.

Charles Baniker
President
RCarz
100 Pioneer Way
Seattle, WA

RCarz knew the batteries were dangerous. And chose to
use them anyway.

The next morning I wake with my sheets twisted around
my legs and my blanket on the floor. I roll over and realize
it's Wednesday. Jade's podcast dropped this morning.

   I turn up the volume. Jade's radio voice sounds louder
and more in charge than her normal, walking-around-the-
neighborhood voice. She starts with my interview, where I
tell her what happened that morning. My eyes sting. Then
she jumps right in: "RCarz knew the specific lithium-ion

batteries in the remote-control cars could overheat and start a fire but decided that a redesign of the product would cost more than dealing with a few lawsuits from injured users. Apparently this is called bean counting. Don't know about you, but as a fellow human, I'm pretty horrified. Despite contrary findings by the fire investigation, RCarz continues to deny responsibility for the accident."

Before signing off, she acknowledges the "fine contributions of Eric Stein."

I wish I could run over to Dani's house and talk to her about the show, but I can't. Not anymore. I'm doing my part to get the company to stop selling the defective toy car. But I've accepted that there's no going back for Dani and me.

She's changed.

And so have I.

40

Forever People

Mom and I are going to the Cape. It was my idea. I want to remember what I loved about the place. About me. I'm kind of scared the accident squeezed out all the good stuff.

Before we leave, I pick up a framed photo of Gigi and me at a Red Sox game. I stare at her face and can almost hear her giant laugh. It makes me wonder how you know which people in your life are your forever people. Sometimes they surprise you. Like the people you think will be here for always leave too soon, and the ones you thought might bail stick around.

I put down the photo, hook the bag Mom helped me pack onto my back, and use the walker to get to the car.

Slow and steady. Just the way I've been practicing with Waylan. I'm almost able to walk across the parallel bars.

This time the ride to the Cape is not filled with baseball stats or Mr. Stein's classic rock music. It's filled with my thoughts and Casey's snores.

As we cross over the Sagamore Bridge, I don't look at my phone. I close my eyes. I want to feel the breeze kissing my cheeks. I want to smell the ocean air. I want to remember the part of me that loved this place.

Instead, I just feel numb and angry.

"Hungry?" Mom asks, startling me.

"Sure," I say.

We pull into the parking lot of Bayview, one of my favorite Cape restaurants, and Casey licks my face. Ever since I came home from the hospital, she's been following me everywhere. I think she's watching over me. Kind of like Gigi. I haven't told anyone this, but the other day when I was sitting in Gigi's room and rubbing between Casey's ears, she looked up at me with her beautiful gray eyes and I swear I saw Gigi. It was like she was looking at me *through* Casey. I know this sounds completely crazy. I never really bought into the whole reincarnation thing, but in that moment I *felt* my grandmother's presence. I had goosebumps all up my arms. I was about to say something. Like, *I love you. I miss you. Is that you?*

Then Casey sneezed and the feeling disappeared.

We've been eating at Bayview since I was little. It's next to a cranberry bog and makes the best Cape Codder sandwich, with turkey, stuffing, homemade cranberry sauce, and gravy. We get a table outside, right in front of a birdhouse shaped like a castle, and when the waitress comes over, we order two Cape Codders.

"Jade's story is going to make a difference," Mom says, drinking her cranberry seltzer. "It'll be hard for the company to ignore the podcast. I'm proud that you talked to her. I know that sharing so publicly, getting the story out there so it will make a difference for others, wasn't easy." She rests her hand on my back.

It feels good. And as much as I want to freeze this moment, it's not mine to keep.

"It was really all Eric. I may have been the one to speak to Jade, but Eric set it all in motion. He stepped up in a big way." I pause. "And never bailed."

Even when I let Meadow call him a loser.

Even when he wasn't invited to my party.

Even when I was a jerk.

I twirl his lucky coin in my pocket.

A blue jay sits on the castle feeder and looks at me likes she's listening to my heart. She bobs her head and hops onto the back of my chair. Stares at me, then flies away.

When we're done, I want to go to Mayflower Beach. It's

low tide. We park but don't go out onto the powdery sand. It's too unsteady for me to walk on yet. But from the parking lot I can see the stretch of milky beach. Casey barks at the dogs swimming in the ocean. I notice two kids fishing and remember this one time when Eric and I were in fourth grade. We tied a piece of cooked chicken to a string that we hooked to a clothespin and dangled from the jetty. We waited all afternoon for something to bite. Ended up catching a crab and an old boot.

That feels like a different lifetime, a different place, a different Cape.

When we leave, I ask Mom to head to Scargo Lake. I stare out at the lake that's oddly shaped like a fish. Eric and I spent so much time stomping through the marshy bottom here, holding our nets and catching and releasing tadpoles in the reeds. We even named one Zipper, and each time we found a tadpole, we were sure that it was him.

We watch the sun set over the lake. Then Mom turns to me: "Why did you want to come here today? I mean, I love a great Cape Codder, but it's a long way to drive for a sandwich." She smiles.

"I wanted to remember the good stuff about the Cape." I pause. "And about me. You know, before—"

—the accident.

Before I messed up everything.

Before. Before. Before.

"Did it help?" Mom asks.

I nod.

On the way home I ask my mom to make one last stop at Lulu's Gift Emporium, where I pick out a blue Cape Cod sea glass charm for my no-longer-empty bracelet.

41

My Own Kind of Superpower

I may never be the lead in the school musical, but singing in the shower is most definitely my jam. I hum and sing and towel-dry while the bathroom fills with steam.

As I get dressed I decide it's time to talk with God again. I've been thinking about this for a while. A way to say thanks. So I put on my old jeans and Captain America T-shirt and start.

Okay, you held up your end of things.

Dani's going to be okay.

The accident wasn't my fault.

And even if I can't fix things between Dani and me, I kind of feel like I owe you.

I take Tony and Stark out of their cage and let them race around my room in their plastic ball.

I assume you're busy and thought maybe I could help. See, I kind of have a superpower.

Now, before you go guessing, it's not mind reading or invisibility, super strength or flight. It's my own thing. I see stuff differently.

Which is a good thing.

Even if not everyone gets it.

And I don't give up on stuff or people.

Another good thing.

I look at my gerbils racing to nowhere and think of Dani. Even though I miss her, I know she's going to be okay. And hopefully, with the podcast out now, RCarz will stop selling the defective remote-control car so no one else can get hurt.

A happy feeling slips in.

Still not sure how this is supposed to work between us, but I just wanted to say thanks.

I sit on the floor with Tony and Stark, grab my notebook, and begin to write the comic I tried writing when Dani was at baseball camp. Now I know that it's about a superhero kid named Sideways. A kid with his own superpower. His real name is Mickey. He's short with brown hair, loves lots of different stuff, is messy and smart but not great at school. What he *is* great at is solving problems. I write and draw for a while.

The story spills out of me surprisingly easily. Which has never happened with any writing ever before.

And I like it.

Which has also never happened.

Then my phone buzzes. It's Rachel. She wants to meet.

I don't, but I know I can't keep ignoring her.

I put my comic away and use the body spray Aunt Josie gave me. No matter how I feel about seeing her again, I don't want to smell like my breakfast burrito. Then I grab my backpack and head out to meet Rachel at the stone wall.

When I get there, she's sitting on the ledge, working on today's *Clippings* crossword puzzle. I toss my backpack on the ground and shove my hands in my pockets.

She shows me the crossword. Almost everything's filled in with purple. "I'm stuck on the last two," she says.

I nod.

"I heard Jade Zhang's podcast. Congratulations. You did it," she says, hopping off the wall.

I step back.

"Come on, Eric, don't be mad." She gathers her hair, winds it in a bunlike thing, and clips it on the top of her head. "I'm sorry I used the accident for the private-school application. My dad just thought it would look good and increase my chances of getting in."

I shake my head and all the frustration about her stupid essay churns in my stomach.

"The thing is, he wasn't wrong." She smiles. "The essay's

great." She pauses and her eyes fall to the grass. "He also thinks you're making a big deal out of nothing."

"Is that what you think?" I ask.

She doesn't answer.

"You included stuff in your essay that I told you in private. It's like you pretended what happened to Dani and me also happened to you. But it didn't. You weren't even there."

"Why do you care? It's not like Dani's been a good friend. She called you a loser," Rachel says.

I ignore her hurt-laced words. "Technically Meadow did, but that has nothing to do with this," I say. "You used me and then lied about it."

Her eyes catch mine and her voice softens. "I didn't use you. I borrowed your story. There's a difference."

"Not to me."

"Come on. You know how parents can be. He's my dad, Eric. He was trying to help." She moves closer to me.

"I'm sorry, Rachel, but I can't do this anymore," I say. Then I turn and walk away from her and the stone wall.

Because as much as I like the smell of honeysuckle, the truth still matters.

42

Spinning

My hair may be short and my body may not work the way I want it to. I may not have it all figured out or know where any of this will lead. But Waylan's right: I finally know who I am and who I want to be in my heart.

And maybe for now, that's enough.

I grab my phone from my yellow desk, lean it against a stack of books, and hit Record.

"Hey, friends. Dani here, from Say It or Do It. I know I'm usually a duo with Meadow, but today I'm going solo. So hear me out. You want the truth, right? Here it is.

"Eric's not a loser. He's my friend. Sure, he's a goofball who loves Iron Man. A choice I've told him is crazy compared to Mystique, my personal favorite comic book character of all time. But he's *my* goofball, and I've been a jerk. I should have stood up for him sooner.

"It's been a hard ride since the accident, but I can't keep using that as an excuse. I can't sit silently and let others speak for me.

"That ends today.

"Eric, I'm sorry.

"There you have it. The whole truth from Dani Meyer."

I turn off the video and hit Upload.

I reach for my walker, and my phone immediately buzzes. I sigh, because no matter how good I've gotten at using the walker, I still haven't mastered doing it while talking on the phone.

I sit back down and answer my phone. Casey cuddles next to me.

"I can't believe you made a video without me." It's Meadow.

"How'd you even see it?"

"We're both on the account. Remember? I get a notification anytime you post."

I hear music in the background. "Oh, right." I rub Casey's nose.

"I thought we were doing this together," she says.

"I had to fix things, Meadow. That stuff you said about Eric wasn't cool."

"It was a joke."

I glance in the mirror. The girl looking back at me shakes her head and takes a big breath. "It wasn't funny, Meadow."

"When did you lose your sense of humor?"

An uneasy feeling swishes in my stomach. "I don't get you. Don't you feel bad about any of it? Eric? Your brother? Your sister?"

The phone goes dead quiet. "This has nothing to do with Millie or Remi," she snaps. Then another long stretch of nothing. "Look, I'm sorry," she says in a softer voice.

I sigh. "Okay."

Followed by an uncomfortable silence.

"I've got to go," I finally say and hang up the phone. Ever since Meadow's confession about lying, things have been weird, and not good weird. Just weird weird. In a lot of ways, Meadow reminds me of Mystique, always shape-shifting to blend in. Works great in a superhero, less great in a friend.

Then I think about me and all the shape-shifting I've been doing. I ask Mom to stop at Anna's Bakery on the way to school. I pick up a dozen of Eric's favorite glazed donuts, and one Boston cream for me.

Mom drops me at school. I steer my wheelchair over the cracked sidewalk. I can do it mostly myself now and am thankful the school has smooth hallways. Less thankful that I haven't made it all the way across the parallel bars yet.

I glide down the hall, looking for Eric. I need to give him my apology donuts. I need to tell him I'm sorry.

But I don't see Eric, or anyone else. It's early, so the school's still mostly empty.

I decide I'll find him later.

I head directly to first period since there's no homeroom today. After a bit, the rest of the kids trickle in. Mr. Rhodes is wearing a SpongeBob SquarePants tie, a present from his five-year-old son. I kind of love it. As he turns to write something on the board, I wipe my hand across my forehead and realize I'm sweating. I look around. No one else even looks hot. Not even Jeremy, and he's a sweater.

The kid to my right says something to me.

I don't hear him.

My hands tingle.

He repeats whatever he was saying, but his voice sounds muffled.

Mr. Ari claps his hands.

I turn toward him. My body feels like it's on fire.

Mr. Ari needs to open a window.

I raise my hand.

I'm so hot. Even the soured spit making its way up my throat is hot.

Kind of wishing I ate breakfast, or at least my donut.

"Yes, Dani?" Mr. Ari says.

His SpongeBob tie melts like a color-wheel spinning.

And spinning.

And spinning.

My hands tingle and shake, but when I look down, they're on my lap, not moving.

I try to answer Mr. Ari. "I'm, um—"

I feel fuzzy. Like cotton candy.

Dizzy.

Now everything is black.

And.

Cold.

43

Just a Mistake

I watch the video.

She's sorry.

Then I watch it again to make sure Meadow's not in the background laughing, that it's not some kind of a joke's-on-you thing. But it isn't. It's just Dani.

My brain is so happy it can't think, and I end up being late for school, because I forget my English homework and need to run home and get it. This would have been strike three for not remembering my homework, and I don't want detention.

I'm sprinting back to school, hoping my black T-shirt hides any sweat stains I'm sure are happening, when I see

Leo and JJ, his older brother, who's screaming at him. Not like you-forgot-your-homework-again yelling but more like you're-a-worthless-waste-of-air yelling.

I know the difference.

As I pass them JJ spews more venomous words. My eyes connect with Leo's, and in that moment I feel bad for the kid I hate.

When I get to class, I'm still thinking about Leo as Ms. Walker's explaining the etymology of the word *lollipop*. I find my desk, and the classroom phone rings. Ms. Walker answers it, speaks softly, hangs up, and walks over to my desk. "Eric, that was Principal James. He'd like to see you in his office."

"Why?" My mouth feels dry.

"He didn't say."

I leave class with a sinking feeling in my gut. My shoes stick to the floor as I drag myself down the hallway.

When I get to the office, Principal James is standing by his door, waiting for me. He's not working or on the phone or rummaging through papers on his desk. He's just waiting. Waves of nausea roll across my body.

"What did I do?" I ask.

"Nothing, Eric. Your parents are on their way to pick you up."

"Why?"

I clench my teeth.

In a gentle voice, Principal James says, "Dani passed out in class and has been taken to the hospital."

I struggle to focus. "No. She's fine," I explain. "She recorded a video this morning. I saw it. She was totally normal."

This is just a big misunderstanding.

Then my parents walk into the office.

"Mom, what's going on?" I ask, desperate for a different explanation.

"We don't know anything yet," Dad says, tugging his beard.

"You're all wrong. Dani's fine. This is just a mistake," I say, trying to convince myself.

Mom hugs me tight and says nothing for a minute. Then, softly, she says, "We all love Dani."

My body floods with fear. In my mind there was no going back. Once Dani was okay, she was supposed to stay that way.

My parents and I drive to the hospital in silence. We don't see Alice. We settle into the horribly familiar waiting room with the magazines, Disney music, tissue boxes, and smell of old coffee.

I don't want to be back here, hoping and praying Dani's going to recover. Especially now. I saw the video. She's sorry. I'm sorry. I need to tell her that I'm not mad. That I forgive her.

I walk to the chapel, on purpose this time. It's empty. I slide into a velvet seat at the end of an aisle. I clasp my hands together and squeeze my eyes closed. My leg jitter bobs.

I'm back. I'm sorry for anything I've ever done wrong. I'm sorry I told Zoe there were no more chocolate chip cookies and then ate the last one. I'm sorry Tony and Stark's cage might not be so clean. I'm sorry I stink at remembering. But, I promise, I'll do anything for Dani to be all right.

I can't think of anything else to say, so I thank God, get up, and wind my way back to the waiting room.

After a few hours and many failed attempts to crush my time on *Crossword King,* Alice finds us. I jump up, almost knocking over the magazine table. "Is Dani okay?"

"She's going to be fine," she says.

"Thank goodness," Mom whispers.

"What happened?" I ask.

Alice's voice goes soft. "Dani fainted. The doctor said she was dehydrated and likely anxious and overheated. She's all right now. They just want to keep her overnight to keep an eye on her in light of everything."

"Are you sure?" My fists stay clenched in tight balls by my sides.

Please be sure.

"Yes," she says, her voice soft.

Slowly I release my grip.

"Can I see her?" I ask.

Alice nods. "She's asking for you."

"Eric, you go with Alice," Mom says. "We'll wait here."

I follow Alice to Dani's room. We pass Nurse Reed, who waves. I wave back, but the truth is, I never wanted to see him again. The door to Dani's room is open. Alice leaves to talk to the doctor, and I walk in. Dani's face is pale and she's hooked up to the annoyingly familiar beeping monitor.

"Hey," I say, sitting in the chair next to Dani's bed.

"Hi," she says. She raises the top of her bed with the button so she's facing me. "I'm sorry for—" Long pause. "Well, I'm sorry for all of it."

"I saw the video." I put my hand on my knee, hoping to calm the jitter bob.

"I've been a jerk," Dani says.

I don't disagree.

"A big jerk."

I nod. "I'm sorry, too. You told me to let it go, and I didn't. Couldn't, really." I open a bag of M&M's, take a handful, and give some to Dani.

"But that's the thing. You were right this whole time. If we'd done nothing, nothing would have happened. Now, because of all the stuff you did, people know my story, and hopefully no one else will be able to buy the stupid, defective remote-control car."

"I was, um, worried that maybe you'd shape-shifted permanently."

Dani smiles. "Nope, it was temporary." She sighs. "Look,

if I'm being honest, all this feels really scary, but I finally know that I'm going to find my way back to okay. Whatever that looks like." She pauses and takes a sip of her water. "I also know what Meadow said, and what I didn't say, and I don't believe any of that. None of this was your fault."

I blow out a giant breath.

Not my fault.

Before I can launch into my happy dance, Meadow's at the door.

I freeze.

"Can I come in?" She sounds nervous.

I look at Dani, who looks at Meadow and is silent.

"Why are you here?" I ask, finding the courage to say the things I usually don't.

"I want to make sure Dani's all right." She turns to Dani. "I'm sorry again that I wasn't honest." Then back to me. "And I shouldn't have said that stuff about you or, um, called you a loser."

I'm quiet.

"Okay if I stay?" Meadow asks.

I don't answer, just hand her my open bag of M&M's.

44

Blue Butterfly

Dr. Jeffries comes in the next morning with good news. I can leave the hospital *and* get my cast off.

"Thank goodness," Mom says, her hands clasped in front of her.

He then reminds me to drink lots of water and stay hydrated. Other than that, he says, I'm doing a great job, and if I continue improving at this rate, pitching is a "definite possibility" next year. I'm not sure what *definite possibility* means, but a happiness I haven't felt in a long while seeps in.

As Mom and I head home, I run my hand down the new

black boot that's covering my right leg and wiggle my toes. It feels funny, but in a good way.

We pull into the driveway and there's a letter from Meadow sitting in our mailbox. She must have dropped it off, because there's no stamp, just pink stationery with a blue butterfly in the corner.

Dani,
I've done some stuff, said some not-okay things, and lied. I know I apologized already, but there's more I want to say. See, I'm trying to do things differently now. I'm working on owning my part of the mess I made and being better.

I didn't want to tell you this before, but a while back my mom sent me to see Dr. Raheim. He's a therapist. I didn't want to go at first. Now I kind of like him. He's nice. Not as cute as Waylan, though. :)

The honesty letter was his idea. My first one was to Remi. My second one is to you.

Now, for the honesty thing. This part is hard for me. It feels cringey, but here goes. I guess you could say lying's been a part of me for a long time. I never meant to hurt anyone. To me, lies were like spices I added to the truth so I could feel like I was something. You see, Remi's always been the super smart one.

Millie's the super cute one. And me, well, I'm not super anything.

I'm not telling you this to excuse what I did, just to explain. That's what Dr. Raheim said I should do. I'm really sorry.

Your friend (hopefully),
Meadow

After I read the letter, I think about the not-great stuff I did to Eric and call Meadow. "I got your letter."

"I'm sorry for everything," she says.

"I know." I exhale.

"Do you forgive me?"

"No more lying," I say, staring at my newly freed leg.

"I promise." She's silent for a minute. Then she says, "Are we, you know, like, still friends?"

"Why do you even care? I mean, you have tons of friends."

"You're different. It matters to me. So, are we, you know, friends?"

"We're not *not* friends," I say.

"Got it. You won't regret this. I promise."

After we hang up, I call Eric and try to return his lucky coin. He tells me to hold on to it. Something about him having his own superpower now. I don't ask what he's talking about. I'm just happy to have the coin a bit longer.

I twirl it in my palm. I'm in Gigi's room. Mom said we're going to start going through it together soon. Casey joins me on the honey-colored bedspread, smelling like wet dog mixed with cucumber. Mom just gave her a bath. She looks up at me, and that's when it happens again: I see her. Or feel her.

Chills race up my spine. "Gigi, um, hey."

Casey licks my face.

"So this is weird. But if it's you, I want you to know I miss you."

Casey shakes her wet body.

I pause and she looks at me.

"I love you. And I know that I'm more than baseball." A tear falls onto my blanket.

I hug my dog.

My Gigi.

My dog.

Then I tell her that she doesn't have to worry. That I'm working hard with Waylan at physical therapy. That I'm getting stronger and drinking iced tea with a speck of honey and lemon—just like we used to do together.

Casey curls into a ball next to me and falls asleep.

I look at my leg. I feel like I'm closer to being back to me. Closer to baseball. Even my shoulder and hand are stronger. I'm better at using a fork, buttoning my pants, writing, and typing on the computer.

Today I text Eric and ask him to meet me at PT after school.

When he gets here, I'm sitting across the room in front of the parallel bars. I wave.

"What's going on?" Eric asks, making my mom's worry face. "You okay?"

I nod. "Watch this," I tell him.

"Ready?" Waylan asks me.

"Ready," I say, taking a deep breath.

I stand up. I wobble at first, then find my balance. I haven't walked all the way across the parallel bars since the accident. But today is the day, and I want Eric to be here with me.

I hold my breath, grip the bars, and squeeze the muscles in my stomach like Waylan said, to steady me.

"Slowly now. One step at a time. You can do it." Waylan's voice is strong. "Whenever you're ready, let's dance." He taps his phone and his best of the 80s playlist sounds in the background.

I take one step and then another and another. My steps are small. I inch forward slowly. Then lean awkwardly to one side. Eric moves to help me, but Waylan motions him to sit back down. I steady myself, and then I slowly walk across the parallel bars. Then sit in a chair that Waylan has placed at the end. Waylan and Eric clap wildly.

"Awesome!" Eric says.

"Thanks."

He gives me a high five. "Congrats. I mean it."

Eric spends the rest of the session helping with my exercises while Waylan coaches us both. I learn how to use the forearm crutches. We laugh and I feel happy. Like hot-dogs-with-relish happy.

45

No One Will Notice

"The Cobras are playing the Grizzlies at school soon. It's the final home game of the season. Want to go?" I'm sitting at Dani's kitchen table and ante up three green M&M's. I'm down two games in Gin Rummy, but think I can pull out a win with this hand.

"Not really," Dani says, taking the face-up card in the middle and sliding it into the card holder I made for her out of an empty tinfoil box.

Dani hasn't gone back to the baseball field since she bailed on hanging with the team over six weeks ago. Not to watch a game. Not to visit the team. And now it's my job to convince her to go.

Last week Coach Levi pulled me aside during lunch. He said the baseball team had planned a surprise tribute to Dani and they needed me to get her to the game. Dani's mom would be at the field, but everyone agreed it'd be less obvious if I got her there.

"You have to return sometime," I say, eating the next M&M.

"I know."

"So why not this game? No one will even notice you're there." I hold my breath, praying that doesn't sound like I'm part of some master plan. "What do you say?"

"I say you can be a giant pain."

"I'll take that as a yes." I smile.

She smiles back.

We leave after I win the next hand. And when we get to the baseball field, the bleachers are packed and there's a huge banner hanging across the scoreboard: THIS GAME IS IN HONOR OF OUR FRIEND DANI MEYER.

"No way," Dani says.

Coach Levi steps up to the microphone that's set up on the pitching mound. Alice is next to him. "This game is dedicated to a friend of ours who has recently fought and conquered quite an uphill climb. Dani Meyer never gave up. She's a fighter, a friend, and our teammate. We're so proud of her."

The crowd of kids and parents stands and breaks into thunderous cheers. I see Zoe, Aunt Josie, and my parents clapping.

Dani turns to me.

"You knew?" she asks as Casey runs over to her.

I nod.

She smiles, crutches her way over to her mom and hugs her, then slowly turns to Coach Levi.

The crowd chants, "Dani, Dani, Dani, Dani!"

Coach wraps his large arm around Dani's shoulder and says something in her ear. Dani nods and moves toward the microphone. Casey follows and the place fills with silence.

Dani pans the field slowly. It takes her a minute, but then she says, "I'm so happy to be here. I could never have fought so hard without the help and support of my family and friends." She looks my way. "Thanks for being part of my team."

The bleachers roar with applause.

Dani and Casey join her mom, Coach Levi, my parents, Zoe, Aunt Josie, and me as we move off the field.

After the game, the baseball team swarms around Dani. I lean in and tell her I'll meet her outside. I want her to have this moment. I grab popcorn from the concession stand and see Leo walking toward me. I never said anything to anyone about that morning I saw his brother screaming at him. I just felt bad for him in a way I never thought I would.

As he gets closer I don't reroute, and I don't look away.

No worries, God.

I've got this.

His shoulder grazes mine. He glances at me. I glance

back. He says nothing. No obnoxious not-funny joke. No outright mean thing. He just keeps walking.

I smile.

I may still have skinny arms, but I've changed.

And the world knows it.

46
Back to Me

Six months have passed since the tribute, and a lot has happened. I'm stronger and much of the time walking without crutches. I've even graduated to the hardest PT band for my hand.

The podcast got tons of media attention. Jade Zhang came over one morning in April and told us she learned that the CPSC had fined RCarz and issued a recall of the defective remote-control car. That meant that RCarz had to stop making the cars and notify all the people who bought them and all the stores that were selling them to return them because they were dangerous.

We did it!

All I want now is to move on.

Not back to the mound but back to baseball. I'm announcing the team's spring games.

And last week Mom and I started going through Gigi's things. There were laughs and tears and lots of cookies. It was hard, but we were doing it together. I even found a charm in Gigi's wooden jewelry box. Mom's eyes lit up when she saw it. I added it to my bracelet. It's a gold heart, to remind me to always follow mine.

When I walk into the kitchen, Eric's waiting for me with a Boston cream donut. "You okay?" he asks.

I nod.

Today is two years since I said my forever good-bye to Gigi.

Eric opens his hand and in it are two tickets to the Red Sox game and coupons for hot dogs.

I twirl our lucky coin and know that I've found my way.

Back to us.

Back to me.

Acknowledgments

Hidden Truths is a story about forever people in our lives. Loving them. Forgiving them. Fighting for them.

This book took twenty-two years to write! Lots of grit, perseverance, commitment, reimagining . . . and heaps of heart! It was a story that I loved then and that I love now. Of all the books I've written, this one required the most research, kindness, and gracious input from many. It truly took a village. I am beyond grateful for the people who shared their time, knowledge, and belief in me.

Topping this list is my forever people—my family. Always.

To my husband, James: You are the love of my life, my best friend, my always and forever person! Thank you for believing in me and my stories even when—or especially when—there were cracks in my armor. And thank you for the input on the legal aspects of this story. You have dedicated much of your legal career to protecting children. You inspire me every day. I love you infinity.

Joshua, when I started this story you were in fourth grade and we sat at lunch sharing our hopes and dreams. You confided that you wanted to kiss a girl before your Bar Mitzvah, and I shared that I wanted to get this book published. Only one of those things happened before you turned thirteen. This year we celebrated your thirtieth birthday, and this story has finally found its way into the world. So much love to you and Sophie. I love you both with all my heart. And I am most grateful to you and Sophie for helping me with all things radio and podcast.

Gregory, you were in kindergarten when the idea for this story sprang to life, and now, as it finds its readers, you're twenty-seven! Thank you for cheering me on and believing in me. Thank you for sharing your heart and your truth. Thank you for your input on Eric and his ADHD, and for always being you. So much love to you and Shannon!

Joan, you are not just my sister, but also my BFF and an amazing writing partner. Happy to retreat with you always. To you and Larry, hugs and love and a million thanks.

To Dad and Sandy, and Gia, the parent pack: I love you with all my heart. Thank you for being my biggest supporters and for never hesitating to walk into a bookstore and tell them all about your daughter and the books they should be carrying. Love you!

To Scott and Rena, Daniel and Faith: East Coast/West

Coast, no matter where we are, I'm grateful for you all. I love being your sister. Love being together always.

Andrew, Matthew, Emily, Ben, Jess, Sam, Maddy, Gabe, Gen, Eli, Ari, Asher: I clearly have the best nieces and nephews in the world. Heaps of love to all of you!

Writing friends and forever friends Sarah Aronson and Victoria J. Coe, your input and guidance—and did I say input in making this story come to life—were cherished and invaluable. Thank you. Thank you. Thank you.

To my girlfriends, forever and always, love you huge. Thank you for the walks, the wine, and the love.

To Andrea Cascardi, a million thanks for being my champion, my agent, and my friend. Your thoughtful feedback is matched only by your support of and belief in me, and of my ability to tell a great story. I'm beyond grateful that we are on this journey together.

Wendy Loggia, editor extraordinaire, how lucky I am to be working with you. You have the most wonderful ability to bring out the best in me. My book whisperer! I love working together. Boundless thanks to you, Ali Romig, and Hannah Hill, Jen Bricking and Jade Rector for the gorgeous cover art, Joey Ho for being my rock star publicist, and the incredible team at Delacorte Press and Random House Children's Books, for your support and cheers and love for this story.

A huge thank-you to Dr. Catherine Bergineau, PhD, licensed clinical psychologist, who read and reread the story to ensure that the manifestation of Eric's ADHD was authentic. Dr. Birgeneau earned a bachelor's degree in psychology at Yale University and a master's and doctoral degree in clinical psychology at the University of Massachusetts, Boston. She completed her clinical internship at Harvard University and went on to complete post-doctoral training in neuropsychological testing at a private practice in Cambridge, Massachusetts. Since the completion of her education and training in 2000, Dr. Birgeneau has been working in the Boston area, providing neuropsychological testing, educational consulting, and ongoing therapeutic treatment to adults and adolescents.

Dani's physical and occupational therapy was a big part of her journey. Mountains of gratitude to Dr. Clare Safran-Norton, PT, PhD, MS, OCS, Clinical Supervisor Physical, and Occupational Therapy Ambulatory Service, Brigham and Women's Hospital, Boston, for her input and guidance with Dani's recovery.

Dr. Lance Willsey, family friend and doctor, a million thanks for diving into this story with me and helping understand and navigate Dani's medical situation.

Joe Mohorovic, former commissioner of the Consumer Product Safety Commission, senior managing consultant at ESi, and knower of all things CPSC, I am most grateful for your kindness and your knowledge of the workings of the CPSC and for your dedication to safety and the protection of others.

Nancy Cowles, safety advocate, founder and executive director of Kids in Danger and knower of all things FOIA, thank you for your dedication to the protection of children and your assistance with the information regarding the Freedom of Information Act.

Boyd W. DeMello, Fire Prevention Inspector, Falmouth Fire Rescue Department, a million thanks for sharing your fire and rescue expertise with me, and for all you do to keep so many safe.

Andrew Siff, thanks for not only being my wonderful nephew, but for sharing your experience navigating a brachial plexus injury while recovering from knee surgery and the work-arounds that come with your amazing determination and creativity. Your positivity is truly inspirational.

Jake Willsey, former college and professional baseball player, I am most grateful for helping me with all things baseball. Go, Red Sox!

Laurie Brownstein, my friend, my family, and the one who kept me company on my research trips to the RV park, RV campground, and Falmouth Fire and Rescue station. Thank you for being there! Much love.

To the teachers and librarians who help kids like Dani find their dreams and themselves, and help kids like Eric find their superpowers, a million thanks. The difference you make leaves a forever imprint on the lives you impact and the hearts you touch. I am most grateful.

And to my readers, you inspire me with your heart, bravery, honesty, and strength. Thank you for reading my stories. Know that your superpowers are within you, tucked right beside your dreams. And sometimes obfuscated by doubt. But trust me, they are there. Waiting for you.

With boundless gratitude,

Elly

About the Author

ELLY SWARTZ grew up in Yardley, Pennsylvania. She studied psychology at Boston University and received her law degree from Georgetown University Law Center. Elly lives in Massachusetts and is happily married with two grown sons, a beagle named Lucy, and a pup named Baxter Bean. She is the author of *Finding Perfect, Smart Cookie, Give and Take,* and *Dear Student,* all for middle-grade readers.

ellyswartz.com

Can Autumn give fair advice to everyone
while keeping her identity a secret?

"A heartfelt, authentic book about friendship, courage, and honesty. It's about finding—
and more importantly, owning—your own voice." —LYNDA MULLALY HUNT,
New York Times bestselling author of *Fish in a Tree*

Dear Student

ELLY SWARTZ

Author of *Give and Take*